Sam

A SHADOW OPS TEAM NOVEL

Makenna Jameison

This book is a work of fiction. Names, characters, places, and incidents are the product of the author's imagination. Any resemblance to actual events, locales, or persons, living or dead, is coincidental.

Copyright © 2023 by Makenna Jameison

All rights reserved, including the right of reproduction in whole or in part in any form.

ISBN: 9798865253457

ALSO BY MAKENNA JAMEISON

ALPHA SEALS CORONADO

SEAL's Desire
SEAL's Embrace
SEAL's Honor
SEAL's Revenge
SEAL's Promise
SEAL's Redemption
SEAL's Command

Table of Contents

Chapter 1	7
Chapter 2	14
Chapter 3	24
Chapter 4	31
Chapter 5	39
Chapter 6	48
Chapter 7	54
Chapter 8	61
Chapter 9	68
Chapter 10	82
Chapter 11	90
Chapter 12	100
Chapter 13	107
Chapter 14	112
Chapter 15	121
Chapter 16	126
Chapter 17	133
Chapter 18	148
Chapter 19	157
Chapter 20	163
Chapter 21	168
Chapter 22	176
Chapter 23	188
Epilogue	194
About the Author	201

Chapter 1

"Oh shit," Ava Kincaid muttered, watching as her heavy backpack fell off the park bench and tumbled to the ground, spilling some of the contents. Her passport landed on the sidewalk, along with her guidebook to Paris, subway map, and stash of granola bars. She knelt down, brushing her strawberry-blonde hair back as she attempted to right her belongings.

"Need some help?" a deep voice rumbled. Her ears perked up. He sounded American.

Ava glanced over in his direction, her heart stuttering as she caught sight of the man who remained a respectful distance away. He was tall. Broad. Muscles atop muscles, with a short buzz cut that screamed military. The quirk of a smile on his face was friendly rather than threatening, and she didn't miss the interest in those green eyes. He looked like he spent a lot of time outdoors, his sun-kissed skin a nice complement to his dark hair. Nothing looked as good as the way his shirt hugged his biceps though, his broad shoulders stretching the cotton tee shirt. The guy was ripped.

Ava licked her lips. "Sure. It was my bad for not zipping it back up."

He lifted a shoulder and moved closer. "Happens to the best of us. You're American," he added unnecessarily.

"Guilty as charged."

"I was talking with some French women at a café earlier," he said conversationally as he ducked down, collecting a few of the stray granola bars. A hint of the scent of clean soap filled the air between them, along with something else that was spicy and masculine. She felt her heartbeat speed up. "They pretended not to speak English, but I think they were just messing with me."

Her eyes ran over his torso, an electric current zapping through her as their fingers briefly touched as she took her belongings back. Her hand looked feminine and small compared to his, her skin smooth whereas his showed signs of physical work. "Mmmm. Maybe they were talking about you."

His lips twitched.

"I would have if I'd been there with my girlfriends," she said with a wink.

He chuckled as Ava shoved the last of her things in her backpack, zipping it shut before standing. She struggled to heft the backpack up, and the guy reached out, grabbing it easily with one muscled arm. He set it on the bench, making sure to lean it against the back so it didn't tumble again. "You might need to redistribute the weight. It's top heavy."

"You backpacking yourself?" she asked with

SAM

curiosity.

"No, just spent a good deal of time packing my rucksack in the Army."

"I knew it," she said teasingly, pointing her finger at him. "I had a feeling you were military."

The guy crossed his muscular arms, smiling. His biceps bunched with the movement, and her eyes briefly tracked to them before returning to his face. He was watching her, and she didn't deny she'd been checking him out. The man was hot. His own appreciative gaze on her made Ava feel warm inside. He wasn't obnoxiously gaping at her, but she didn't miss the way his eyes briefly dropped to her cleavage before returning to her face. She kept in good shape, average sized with curves men appreciated. The top she had on clung to her breasts and revealed just a hint of bare skin above her jeans. It wasn't cropped so much as sexy. Short. She had a feeling he'd taken it all in with just a glance at her. He looked like the type of man that didn't miss much.

"I'm Ava," she said, reaching out one hand. His muscled hand clasped her own—not too tightly, but she could feel his leashed strength.

"Sam," he said, the touch of his warm, calloused skin against her own sending shivers racing down her spine. He held her hand a moment too long, and she looked away from his interested gaze only when she heard a child's peal of laughter across the park.

He released her hand, crossing his arms casually again as he smiled. He was a lot taller than she was, but somehow his presence made Ava feel safe. She traveled a lot and always had a good read on people. "Are you here on leave?" she asked, brushing her hair back as it blew slightly in the breeze. His eyes landed on her hand, and she briefly wondered if he was looking for a ring. Did men even notice that type of thing?

He didn't have on a wedding band either—not that she was looking.

"Sort of. My teammates and I had a layover in Paris, but our flight was canceled," he said, his deep voice doing something funny to her insides. "I don't fly out until tomorrow afternoon, so I'm exploring the city today. What about you? Are you traveling with friends?"

"What if I'm married?" she asked boldly.

"No ring. Are you?" he pressed.

"Nope," she said, popping the second syllable. "I'm single. You?"

"One hundred percent available," he said, causing Ava to burst into laughter. She wasn't the type of woman who giggled around a man, but Sam's blunt interest was somewhat refreshing. It was a weekday morning in the middle of a park in Paris. It wasn't like they'd sneak off to the dark corner of a bar together, kissing until they were breathless.

"I'm backpacking across Europe. My bestie and I explored London for a long weekend, but she didn't have enough leave to travel for several weeks. I've got a list of cities to visit before I fly home."

"And where's that?" he asked, his green eyes focused solely on her.

"Manhattan."

"Huh. And what do you do in Manhattan? I figure most jobs won't necessarily grant you weeks of leave. Are you a student?"

"I'm an artist."

"Are you hoping to get inspired on this trip?" he

asked, flashing that smile at her again.

"Absolutely. I'm visiting museums, sightseeing, and marveling at the wonders of the city. Plus, I'm here to drink cheap wine, have some amazing food, and take a French lover."

His husky laughter filled the air around them. "Too bad I'm American."

"Too bad," she agreed. "Otherwise, you might've been perfect."

Sam raised his eyebrows.

"I'm not above a vacation fling," she said flirtatiously. "I don't know you though, and you're leaving tomorrow. It's probably best if we just stay friends."

"Right," he said, his lips quirking. "I wouldn't want to keep you from those Frenchmen. Until you meet this guy, maybe we could explore some of the city together. You don't speak French, do you?"

"Just what I learned in high school," she admitted. "I'm up for exploring some. I'm planning to go to the Louvre later this week but wanted to check out some smaller, local art galleries."

"I'm game."

"Really?"

"Why not?" he said with a shrug. "I didn't have much of a plan—wasn't expecting to be here anyway. Sightseeing in Paris with a beautiful woman isn't exactly a hardship."

"And you're definitely single."

"I'm single," he said with a low chuckle.

"Right. I don't always have the best luck with men, but it's not like we're dating. We're tourists in Paris exploring the city."

"Exactly. And if you get tired of me following you

around, I promise not to be a dick about it. I'll do my own thing and tell my buddies about the pretty girl who ditched me in Paris. C'est la vie."

She shook her head, trying not to smile. Sam was a flirt, but she couldn't deny that she enjoyed the attention. He was handsome as hell, and exploring Paris with him would be more fun than being on her own. "I need to drop my bag off at my hotel first. I checked in yesterday but spent the morning at the laundromat. I'm not paying the exorbitant fees the hotel charges to do the guests' laundry."

"Is your hotel close by?"

"Just a block away," she said, glancing up the street. "I stopped for a bit because the park was so gorgeous. I was going to sit outside at a café with a coffee and then visit the galleries. So, if you want to join me, you're welcome to."

"I'd love to buy you a coffee," he said, his eyes twinkling.

"But—"

"Nope. It's on me. I'll walk you back," he said, nodding in the direction she'd pointed. "We can drop it off and then go exploring. My buddies and I are staying near the airport. We were trying to catch another flight, but it was completely booked."

Sam reached down and easily hefted her backpack onto one shoulder, making it look lighter than she knew it to be. "Is this all you're traveling with?" he asked.

Ava burst into laughter as they began walking down the street. "Of course not. I've got a small suitcase, but I made sure I could carry everything on my flight. I hate checking bags, and it doesn't do me any good to pack luggage so heavy I can't even lift it."

SAM

"Yep. You should've taken me with you on the plane," he said.

She swatted his arm, enjoying the feel of firm muscle beneath warm skin.

"Ouch," he joked.

"That did not hurt," she chastised.

"Not at all," he agreed.

Ava found herself trying to stifle a laugh. "Good thing I found you then—to carry my backpack and all."

"Pretty sure I found you," he commented dryly.

She laughed again, her chest filling with warmth at the way he looked down at her. They continued down the Paris street, and Ava couldn't help but marvel what a perfect day it was. The sun was shining, the birds were chirping, and she was happy. She and her best friend Wren had an amazing time in London, but Ava was an extrovert. She was thrilled to have someone to spend the day with and certainly hadn't expected to meet anyone like Sam. He was fun. Flirty. After they went their separate ways at the end of the day, she hoped she'd have some fond memories of their day together in Paris. If Sam was in the military, she doubted she'd see him again. He could be stationed anywhere, and she wasn't exactly looking for a boyfriend. A hot guy to explore with, however? That she could very much get on board with.

Chapter 2

Sam Jackson strode down the street beside the woman he'd just met, his lips quirking. Ava was animatedly telling him about the sightseeing she'd done in London with her best friend. Her long hair swished as she moved, and he got a whiff of her sexy, floral scent. She was beautiful. Long, strawberry-blonde hair, fair skin, and pretty blue eyes. Ava wore fitted jeans with a tight tank top, and he'd have to be blind to miss her killer curves. The tank hugged her breasts perfectly, her delicate necklaces dangling against her cleavage. She was petite, only coming up to his shoulder, but he had no doubt her body would fit against his perfectly.

Not that he had plans to test out that theory. It wasn't even noon, and they'd agreed to visit some art galleries together, not rip each other's clothes off. Although he planned to hit up some nightclubs later with his buddies, if the day went well, he wouldn't mind ditching them for Ava. He'd be leaving tomorrow, but that wouldn't necessarily stop Ava and him from enjoying an evening together. Or the entire night.

He easily carried her backpack on one shoulder, wondering how she'd lugged it around by herself. He didn't mind holding it and had been amused watching her heft it back onto the park bench. She was so much smaller than him, he couldn't help but feel slightly protective toward her. In his line of work, he was used to keeping people safe. Going after the bad guys, so to speak. Watching out for a beautiful woman as they walked down the city street and carrying her heavy bag wasn't a hardship.

They sure as shit weren't dodging gunfire and taking out a tango.

He scrubbed a hand over his jaw. Ava had assumed he was military, and there wasn't much of a reason to correct her. He'd be on his way to the Middle East tomorrow, meeting up with a contact before bringing in an HVT, or high value target, wanted by the U.S. government. Sam and his friends were part of the Shadow Ops Team. Former Delta Force soldiers, they'd been recruited by their boss when they got out of the military. A mission that went bad with a teammate being held hostage was all that they needed to say goodbye to Uncle Sam. Now they took jobs the government couldn't or wouldn't handle—a covert black ops team that deployed around the world, all under the guise of working for Shadow Security.

"I'm staying right over there," Ava said, gesturing to a boutique hotel, and drawing Sam's attention back to the present.

His gaze flicked to the building on the corner of the Parisian street. The quaint hotel wasn't necessarily one he'd pick, yet it suited her. A little café was across the street, along with several shops on the ground floor of an apartment building. It was the same down the entire block. Charming even. It seemed a safe area for a woman traveling alone, although as they approached her hotel, he didn't like how anyone on the street could simply walk in.

"I didn't think I'd be bringing a man back to my hotel this morning," Ava said, flashing him a saucy grin. Her blue eyes sparkled with mischief, and his eyes briefly dipped to her cleavage as her necklaces gleamed in the sunlight.

Sam made a sound at the back of his throat. Ava was a flirt, but he'd promised himself he'd be good. "To be honest, I'm not sure I've ever walked a woman I just met back to her hotel in broad daylight."

"Midnight more your style?" she quipped.

"I'm no saint, but I don't go hooking up with random women all the time, if that's what you're worried about."

"Of course not. Because we're not hooking up. I still need to take a French lover, remember?" Her cheeks were flushed as she looked up at him, and Sam didn't miss the way her eyes tracked over his chest. He kept in good shape, and while his shirt wasn't overly snug, no one would miss his muscular stature. He sure as hell didn't mind Ava's eyes on him.

"How could I forget? I've been cursing my bad luck of not being French ever since you first mentioned it," he said with a wink.

She laughed, clearly enjoying the way he flirted

SAM

with her, and his gaze dropped briefly to her pink lips. Ava had on some type of lip gloss but otherwise wore minimal makeup. Her cheeks were a pretty shade of pink, but she had fair skin. Any hint of a blush would easily show. He wondered how her strawberry-blonde hair would look against her bare breasts, the long strands teasing her creamy skin. Fuck. He felt his cock twitch and tried to think of something else. She was too damn pretty for him not to have carnal thoughts running through his mind, but he couldn't exactly walk around the city rock hard either.

He reached out to open the door of her hotel, his bare arm brushing against hers. Ava shivered slightly at his touch, and he smiled. She was playful and sexy, but he loved that she wasn't unaffected by him. There was clearly a mutual attraction between the two of them. Sam's hand landed on the small of her back as he guided her through the doors, and he stared at it splayed across her delicate frame for a beat. He could feel the heat of her body beneath the thin tank top, and he noticed the slight hitch of her breath at his touch. She was so damn small and delicate compared to him. Sam felt like he should watch out for her, keeping her safe, but he also wanted to strip her bare and explore every square inch of her.

It was quite the conundrum.

He continued guiding her into the small lobby, towering above her frame. His gaze swept the area out of habit, taking in the other guests and hotel staff. There was a front desk staffed by a lone woman, and no one seemed to be paying attention to who was coming in or out of the building. He lifted his gaze, looking for any security cameras. There was one pointed at the doors at least. No telling how good it was though. An elevator dinged, and as he finished scanning the area, he saw a set of double doors across the lobby leading to a small conference room.

Ava turned toward him, and Sam handed over her backpack, helping to ease it onto her shoulders. "You got it?" he questioned, knowing firsthand how heavy it was. He didn't want to follow her up to her room like some sort of creep, but he also didn't like the idea of Ava carrying it alone.

"Of course," she assured him. "I'm traveling all over Europe. I can make it upstairs with my backpack."

"I'll wait in the lobby. We can head out whenever you're ready."

"Such a gentleman," she teased.

"I can be," he replied, a playful smirk teasing about his lips. Ava's eyes tracked over him again, and Sam nodded toward the elevator. "Go on before I change my mind. We've got the entire day to explore the city together."

"And tonight?" she asked, her pretty blue eyes gazing at him as she wet those pink lips with her tongue.

"I guess we'll find out," he murmured huskily.

"Indeed, soldier," she said before turning and moving smoothly across the lobby, pressing the button for the elevator. Sam's gaze inadvertently dropped to her round ass, and he resisted the urge to groan. He was in so much trouble today.

***

"Monsieur! Mademoiselle! A photo to remember your vacation."

SAM

Ava's gaze slid to the man taking pictures near the Eiffel tower, her small purse clutched in one hand. Sam's arm was casually draped over her shoulders, keeping her warm, his thumb rubbing tiny circles on her skin. It was no wonder the guy thought they were a couple; she was snuggled up against him like they'd always been together.

"Let's have him take our picture," Ava said. "Look how pretty the Eiffel tower is lit up like that. And when will I ever be in Paris again with a hunky man? I'll show these pictures to my grandkids someday."

Sam chuckled but agreed, and Ava handed over her phone. "I'll tip him," Sam said in a low voice, pulling out his wallet. He handed the guy some cash and then shocked Ava by scooping her up into his arms for the picture. She squealed in surprise and was still laughing as they both grinned for the photo.

"Magnifique!" the Frenchman called out. "Ze perfect couple!" he said in his accented voice. "A couple more shots, oui?"

Ava's arm had snaked around Sam's neck, and she could feel his broad shoulders and the muscles in his arms bunching as he held her. He was solid everywhere. Sam had one arm under her legs, the other wrapped around her torso. His big hand was possessively gripping her thigh, and despite the jeans she had on, Ava swore she could feel the heat from his touch burning into her skin. She inhaled his clean scent, combined with a hint of something musky and male. She wanted to bury her face in his neck, basking in his strength and warmth.

She could drown in this man if she wanted to. Sam was attuned to her in a way she couldn't express, and the entire day had felt like something out of a dream.

Ava shivered as he held her for another picture, his body heat seeping into her.

"You're freezing," he murmured.

"You'll keep me warm."

Their eyes locked for a beat, and she could see the question in his. Her gaze dropped to his mouth, those full lips she'd been dying to taste all day tempting her. Sam was hot as hell but still a gentleman, clearly content on letting her set the pace of their flirtations. They held hands, and she'd snuggled up to him without hesitation, but this was something more.

Her breath caught as she met his intense gaze once more, and for the first time all day, she found herself speechless. Without a word, he ducked down slowly, giving her the opportunity to push him away. She didn't though, just breathed him in as he moved closer, their breaths intermingling before his lips finally met hers.

Sam's mouth was soft against hers but knowing. Sure. He was gentle but confident, and he kissed her deeper as the people around them whooped and hollered. Ava swore fireworks exploded at his touch, and raw need began to claw at her. Consume her. It was innocent as far as kisses went, Sam holding her close in the middle of a crowd, but her heart pounded in her chest. She was aware of every part of him—the slight stubble of his jaw, the grip of his thick fingers on her thigh, and the hard muscles of his chest and arms.

The Frenchman holding her phone for pictures was clapping, and Sam eventually broke their kiss, shocking her as he gently kissed her forehead before setting her down. Ava's hand landed on his hard abs as she steadied herself, and the man walked over with her phone. She felt a touch lightheaded and overwhelmed, and she gripped Sam's arm as they both thanked the guy for the pictures. Ava sure the hell hadn't expected to have the most romantic kiss of her life in the middle of Paris.

"Merci," Sam said in his deep voice, taking her hand.

Other couples and families were lining up to pose as well, and he guided her around the group of people. His jaw was set, but he somehow looked as affected as her. That kiss had been... shocking. Intimate and sensual despite the fact they were in public, surrounded by other people. They'd been flirting with each other all day, but the moment Sam had lifted her into his arms, the sparks between them had suddenly ignited. His thumb rubbed over her skin as he held her hand, grounding her. Making her feel safe. They'd shared a moment together that had her feeling all sorts of off-kilter. She wasn't in France to meet a man. He was leaving. Still, she couldn't deny that something real was brewing between them.

Sam cleared his throat. "I already texted my buddies and told them I couldn't meet them tonight." He turned to look at her as they walked away from the group of people taking photographs, his green eyes intense. "What else would you like to do? We already grabbed dinner but could get a drink someplace if you'd like."

She clutched onto his hand, trying to wrap her head around their whirlwind of a day. They'd had coffee that morning and visited the galleries. Grabbed lunch and gone sightseeing. Snapped a ton of photos. Shopped. Enjoyed a delicious dinner. The day was coming to an end, but she couldn't bring herself to say goodbye just yet. Ava didn't do one-night-stands, but she knew deep in her heart that if she didn't spend more time with Sam, she'd regret it. Was she really supposed to say goodbye to this incredible man? He was leaving tomorrow, off on whatever military mission he was involved in, and if she didn't seize the moment, they'd part ways, never seeing each other again.

"Come back to my hotel," she said spontaneously.

He looked surprised, his eyes tracking over her face as they stopped in the middle of the sidewalk. "Are you sure?" he asked, his voice husky.

"Of course, I'm sure," she said, moving closer to him and loving how Sam immediately pulled her into his arms.

He tilted her face up, skimming his fingertips across her cheek as goosebumps rose over her skin. "I'd love to come back to your hotel, but I want to make sure you're comfortable with that. We can find a bar someplace to hang out."

"I know we could, but I want this," she insisted. "I want you to stay with me tonight." Ava let her fingers trail over his forearm, feeling the solid muscle beneath his warm flesh. His jaw ticked. Was he holding himself back from kissing her? Touching her?

"I want this, Sam. Let's go back to my room."

He let out the breath he'd been holding. "Then let's go, princess," he said, his voice gravel. Both big hands moved to her face, holding it gently. Reverently. "There's nothing I want more than to spend the night with you. I'm dying to kiss you again—this time without a crowd of onlookers watching. And after that, I plan to explore every inch of your body."

SAM

Her pussy clenched and nipples hardened at his bold words. "Every inch?" she asked, a smile playing about her lips.

He shifted his hand, his thumb skimming over her lower lip. "Um-hmm," he murmured, ducking lower until his mouth was just beneath her ear. He kissed her softly as she arched into him, her breasts pressing against his chest. His stubble rubbed against her tender skin, and his next words were dirty and full of promise. "Every inch, princess. I'll kiss every inch of your gorgeous body and then let you feel every damn inch of me."

Chapter 3

Sam scrubbed a hand over his jaw, waiting for Ava to come out of the small restaurant adjacent to her hotel. The little shops were all closed for the evening, but she'd ordered something, insisting he wait in the lobby so as not to ruin the surprise. He raised his eyebrows at the bag she was carrying as she came back out, looking all smug and sexy.

"Dessert," she explained, winking at him.

"You're going to be my dessert," he teased, moving closer to brush back some of her strawberry-blonde hair. Her face flushed at his touch, and he loved how he could always read her reactions given her fair skin. She looked eager, which made his chest fill. He was dying to get inside her, to feel her body beneath his own, and to touch and taste her everywhere.

"Oh, trust me, I think you'll enjoy this," Ava replied, licking her pink lips as she unabashedly met

SAM

his gaze.

"Oh yeah?" he asked, his curiosity piquing. His gaze dropped to the bag, wondering what was so special about it.

"Definitely," she said, snatching his hand. "Let's go, soldier. If we've only got one night together, we need to make the most of it."

Sam let her tug him toward the elevator, shaking his head. Ava was a tiny little thing but clearly impulsive and headstrong. He hadn't planned to kiss her earlier in front of the Eifel Tower, but it had felt so right holding her in his arms, he couldn't hold back. And now? He'd been ready for her ever since she asked him to spend the night. He'd be flying out tomorrow, and they hadn't made any plans or promises to see each other afterwards, but tonight?

Tonight would be epic.

Hours later, Sam thought for sure that he'd died and gone to heaven. Ava was wild in bed—a total vixen. She'd had no qualms about her body as he'd stripped her bare, palming and caressing her breasts and sucking on her pretty nipples. His fingers had explored her slick pussy, bringing her to orgasm quickly before he spent the evening devouring her. Sam had tasted her everywhere, kissing and licking her smooth skin before eating her out, listening to her sweet cries of pleasure.

Ava had picked up a decadent chocolate dessert at the restaurant and asked the hotel to send up a bottle of champagne. After feeding each other spoonfuls of chocolate souffle while naked in bed and sipping on the bubbly, she'd grabbed a new paintbrush from her luggage and literally painted his body with chocolate sauce—then proceeded to lick it off. His cock was already hard again recalling the enthusiastic way she'd devoured him.

They'd showered together to clean up and then gone at it again, Sam taking her in multiple positions around her hotel room. Ava's pussy had squeezed his cock so hard, he was sure no other woman would ever compare. They were on fire together—blazing and burning brightly, before finally succumbing to sleep in the early morning hours.

Ava nestled against his body felt right. Sam wasn't a cuddler, but he loved the feeling of this woman in his arms. They'd had little time to talk last night, but he knew her body intimately. Thoroughly. She was an artist who taught a couple of classes in New York and had her paintings in small galleries. She'd told him about the sketchbooks she'd brought to Europe, but they'd been too busy exploring each other for him to flip through it. Sam had spent most of the night buried deep in Ava's delectable body, and after the third or fourth round of lovemaking, he'd realized it would be damn hard to let her go.

"Morning," he said huskily as Ava began to stir, soft and warm against him. *So fucking right.*

"Morning," she replied, a smile creeping over her lips. She was drowsy with sleep but looked so content in his arms, it made his chest clench.

"How'd you sleep?" he asked, letting his hand trail over her skin until he was possessively cupping one breast.

"Mmmm," she said, arching into him. Her ass pressed against his stiffening cock, her full breast spilling over his palm. He kneaded it gently, enjoying the feel of her warm flesh. "I love your hands on me. Inside me, too," she said saucily.

SAM

"My princess is so eager," Sam said, sliding one hand down her flat stomach and cupping her bare pussy. "Are you wet for me, little vixen?" His fingers trailed up her seam before parting her lips, her glistening arousal coating his fingers.

"Sam," she breathed.

"I love the way you say my name," he said, pushing two fingers inside her tight channel as he held her against him. His thumb rubbed her clit, and Ava cried out, already squirming against him. Sam alternated playing with her clit and pushing into her core. She was moaning in no time, and as he increased his attentions, she cried out his name, coming for him once more.

"How am I supposed to let you go?" he asked a few minutes later, after he'd let her come down from the orgasm he'd given her.

Ava rolled over to face him, and his gaze briefly dipped to her bare breasts. "We'll exchange numbers. I still need to text you those pictures. You can remember our adventure in Paris when you're deployed to God knows where."

"I'm not sure exactly when I'll be back in the States," he admitted.

Ava lifted a shoulder. "I'm backpacking around Europe, remember? I won't be home either for a while."

Sam ducked down for a lingering kiss. "I'm only an hour or so north of you."

"Perfect. You can't thrust into me all night with that thing and then take it away," she teased, reaching down to caress his stiffening cock. "You're my new favorite toy."

Sam chuffed out a laugh and rolled onto his back,

easing her on top of him and enjoying the view of her topless and perched on his lap. Her bare pussy rubbed against his stiffening cock, and he shifted, sucking one pretty nipple into his mouth. Ava cried out as he laved at her, Sam smiling against her breast. "You're going to come for me again, princess," he said, his voice rough. "Then we'll shower together before I have to go. I need another glimpse of you wet and kneeling in front of me, my cock in that pretty mouth."

Sam gripped her hips, easily lifting her, and then they both groaned as he filled her with his thick erection, Ava taking every last inch of him. She rocked above him before he rolled them over, his body moving over hers. Their lovemaking was slower and sweeter than last night. He assumed that she was sore and wanted to be gentle, but it was also goodbye. He had an op to fly to and needed to get his head in the game, as much as it pained him to leave this gorgeous woman behind.

"You gonna be okay traveling all over Europe by yourself?" Sam asked an hour later, searching her face and feeling a small twinge of regret that he really did have to go. He was dressed in the same clothes he'd worn earlier, and Ava had on a silky robe over her bra and panties. He'd wanted to groan as she covered herself up after their shower, but he couldn't ravish her all day.

"Of course, I'll be okay. I'll text you before I get back to the States so you know I'm alive."

"Don't go hooking up with any Frenchmen," he ordered.

"Guess that ship has sailed," she teased. "You and your magic dick have cured me of my need for a fling

SAM

with a foreigner."

"All in a night's work," he said with a wink. "I still can't believe you live in Manhattan. I can come down there in no time—then make you come all night again."

"Is that a promise?" she asked, those blue eyes sparkling as she pressed closer against him. Ava undid the belt of her silky robe, letting it fall open so he could see her lacy black lingerie. His cock was already stiffening again, pressing against her stomach, and he kissed her, letting his hands roam.

"You're trouble, princess, but exactly the kind I like to get wrapped up in." He brushed back a strand of her hair and ducked down for one last tender kiss, closing the robe around her and tying the sash before he needed to open the door of her hotel room and leave. As much as Sam loved staring at Ava, he didn't want everyone on the entire floor to see her in that sexy lingerie.

"Call me," she said, lifting her hand to her ear, mimicking a phone. "And good luck wherever you're going. Be careful."

"Text me those pictures. And stay safe, my little vixen. I'll see you soon."

***

Ava: Just made it to Amsterdam. Museums are amazing! Can't believe all the people in the Red Light District. My hotel room feels a bit lonely though.

***

Ava: OMG. Backpacked to Belgium, and I might gain

ten pounds here. Food is incredible. Not as amazing as the chocolate I licked off your dick though. ;)

***

Ava: Wow. I thought for sure that last text would get your attention. Guess deployment sucks. I'm flying back to the States next week. Call me when you're home. Can't wait to meet up. xxx

***

Ava: Giving this one last shot in case you didn't get my texts while overseas. I'm back in NYC living my regular life. My bed would look good with you in it though.

Chapter 4

One year later

"I'm telling you, Ava, this is a good thing. You're the impulsive one," Wren said, staring pointedly at her best friend. "Usually, I'm telling you to slow things down. It feels right to move in with Luke. I know you have doubts, but he's not his asshole friend. You know that."

Ava blew out a breath, looking at the remaining boxes in the apartment. The apartment her best friend was currently moving out of in order to shack up with the guy she'd met in Mexico. And not just any guy—a great one. Luke was nothing like the asshole she'd slept with in Paris and never heard from again.

Until Mexico.

Wren had met Luke down in Cancun while searching for her missing teenage sister. Ava had rushed down without thought to help her best friend.

The moment Wren told her Lily had possibly been kidnapped and trafficked, Ava had promised to come help. To kick ass and take names. And she'd been in the resort all of two minutes when the team of men also searching for Lily appeared in the lobby. Luke had been at the front, his gaze fixed on Wren.

And behind him? Sam. The guy who'd ghosted Ava a year ago. Who'd made love to her all night long in Paris, kissed her tenderly goodbye the next morning, and then disappeared. Never responded to her texts. Never called. Never came looking for her in Manhattan, despite the fact he knew her artwork was displayed in galleries there and she'd be easy enough to find, especially for a man in his line of work.

Ava had even called him once, a month after she'd gotten back to Manhattan, leaving a message and inviting him down to the city.

He hadn't responded.

She'd known with absolute certainty that he was blowing her off after that.

Ava's gaze slid to the door of Wren's mostly-empty apartment. Luke and his friends had shown up with a moving truck and the muscle to haul Ava's entire life to Luke's house upstate. Ava had finished packing up the kitchen, wrapping each plate and cup in bubble wrap. The space felt empty now with Wren's possessions all in boxes or on a moving truck. The men had hauled all of the big things out in no time. They weren't in the military either. They were part of some secretive team that handled missions around the world for the government. Sam was former military. He hadn't exactly lied, but he hadn't told her the truth either.

And he'd been too much of a damn coward to text

SAM

her back and say sorry, not interested.

"Ava?" Wren asked.

Her eyes landed back on her best friend. "Of course, I'm happy for you. I'm just still in shock that an awesome guy like Luke is friends with such a dick."

"If it makes you feel any better, Luke agrees that Sam handled things poorly. I think his exact words were that Sam has a lot of groveling to do."

Ava bristled. "He doesn't need to grovel because after today, I don't plan to see him ever again."

"Yeah," Wren said wryly. "Easier said than done."

Ava rolled her eyes, knowing her best friend was right. If they ever did anything as a group, Sam would be there. He'd probably stay away if she asked him to, but that would just make her look like a bitch. He might've been the one who'd wronged her, but everyone would have expected her to move on.

Which of course she had.

Sam himself walked through the door at that exact moment, brushing off his hands and looking damn lickable in a snug tee shirt and worn jeans. Work boots. He was still hot as hell, and as he raised his eyebrows at Ava watching him, she looked away, feeling hurt all over again. He knew every square inch of her body, had held her tightly against him while she cried out his name, and he couldn't even give her the courtesy of replying to a text.

Wren promptly grabbed a box and hustled out, ignoring Sam's offer to carry it and leaving the two of them alone. Ava busied herself with examining the remaining boxes, inspecting the cardboard. Gotta make sure they were labeled properly and all that.

"You gonna ignore me forever, princess?" Sam

asked, and she could feel him staring at her from across the room.

Ava cleared her throat. "Ignore you? That's kind of like the pot calling the kettle black, huh?"

"Yeah. I deserve that."

Ava looked over at him in surprise.

He scrubbed a hand over his jaw, blowing out a sigh. "I tried to apologize in Mexico," he said quietly, moving closer. "I should've treated you better than I did last year, and I know it. For what it's worth, I'm sorry."

She swallowed and looked up into his green eyes from the six feet of space that separated them. Eyes that had gazed into hers while she was pinned beneath him, his large body moving over her own and worshiping her like she was meant to be his.

She shrugged. "Too little, too late. It stung when you never bothered to reply to my texts or offer an explanation, but I'm a big girl. I moved on."

"I'm sorry if I hurt you," he said, actually having the decency to look remorseful.

She crossed her arms, nailing him with an annoyed glare. "An apology a year ago would've been nice. What was the issue anyway? Why pretend that we'd stay in touch? We could've parted ways the next morning knowing we'd never see each other again. Were you just not able to say that to my face?"

He shoved his hands into his pockets, briefly glancing down at the ground before looking back up and pinning her with his stare. "It was me. It's sounds cliché, but it's the truth. I wasn't in Paris looking to meet a woman. I wasn't looking to date or find a girlfriend. It was a brief stopping point on an op. A layover that wasn't even supposed to happen."

SAM

"Got it," she said icily.

"Our night together was amazing," Sam said softly. "I remember every damn moment. The timing was shit because I was flying out and needed to focus on the mission. I had to compartmentalize everything and get the job done. We were gone for several weeks, and then it felt like too much time had passed. I thought maybe it was best just leaving things as a great memory. I did plan to stay in touch with you when we said goodbye."

"Did you consider my feelings at all? Or was it just what worked best for you?"

Sam stilled, her words seeming to sink in.

"You could've at least texted me back. Said thanks for the pictures now have a nice life. I wondered if you were okay," she said, hating the emotion that crept into her voice. "I was worried, and here you were just a massive dick—no jokes about your dick," she added, noticing his lips quirk.

"Not at all," he agreed.

Ava's gaze slid to the door as she heard people coming, but they moved down the hall, continuing on their way to another apartment.

"I should've handled things differently. You deserved better than that. And you're right. I should've considered your feelings. We did really have a job though, and after weeks had passed, it just seemed easier to move on."

Tears pricked at the corners of her eyes, and Ava clenched her jaw. She wouldn't give him the satisfaction of seeing her upset. It was just one night. A vacation fling. Promises from a complete stranger that should've meant nothing. Ava should've known better than to trust him—to think it was anything real. She'd invited him back to her hotel in Paris with no expectations. But after that night? Their heated kisses goodbye the next morning?

She'd been positive she'd see Sam again.

"Right. You gotta do what's easiest for you," she said tightly. Ava turned away, inspecting the boxes again, her skin prickling with awareness. Sam hadn't moved, and she felt him watching her. Assessing. She'd fallen for him hard in Paris. She wouldn't make the same mistake twice.

"So, what's this about Cairo? You're moving there for the summer?" he asked, clearly in no hurry to get back to help load the moving truck.

The others hadn't returned yet, and Ava had a feeling that Wren was keeping them away. Ava had avoided Sam as much as she could since their run-in south of the border. He'd set her world off-kilter just by reappearing in her life, and she hated the uneasiness that wound through her anytime he was near. Sam wouldn't hurt her in the physical sense, but emotionally? She drew in a shaky breath. She had no doubt he could shatter her heart.

"I am moving there," she said. "You heard me earlier. I was commissioned to do some sculptures. It's an amazing opportunity for me that I couldn't turn down."

"There's a lot of instability in Egypt right now. Did you research it before accepting the job?" he asked.

"I'm not sure how that's any of your business," Ava said, turning to glare at him. Sam was still standing there looking stupid hot and being so damn polite. He had some nerve to act all nonchalant now—like he hadn't literally been inside her body.

SAM

Touched her everywhere. Pretended she didn't even exist afterwards.

"I want to make sure you're safe, princess," he said huskily, the words causing her heart to race.

"Don't call me that," she said, growing flustered. "We're not in bed together. We're not a couple. We're not anything." Her voice grew louder, and she hated that he was getting a rise out of her. He looked so damn unaffected by it all.

Sam's gaze briefly raked over her. No doubt he had the same memories that she did. Ava hated that he knew her intimately, in a way most people never would. He deserved no part of her.

"Fair enough," he said, his voice gruff. "But anyone traveling overseas needs to take precautions, especially a single woman."

"How do you know I'm single?"

He shrugged, looking slightly sheepish for the first time. "I might've asked Luke about you. Found out what you've been up to over the past year."

"Charming," she muttered. "Why talk to me yourself when you can gossip with your friends? Did you tell them that we slept together, too?"

He scrubbed a hand over his jaw. "Not when they knew who you were, but yeah, I might've mentioned I met a woman in Paris. My head wasn't in the game when we landed. My teammates all knew something was up. I had to compartmentalize—put that night behind me and focus on the op."

Ava's jaw ticked. Nothing like texting him during her travels, assuming they'd meet up back in New York, and finding out that he'd literally pushed her out of his mind. "Well, whatever. Let's finish helping Wren and Luke. I'll be leaving soon anyway, and we won't have to see each other again after today."

He remained where he was as Ava brushed past him, heading out the door. She felt the heat from his muscular body, the clean, musky scent that was pure Sam. She needed to get out of there—to breathe, to scream in frustration, to do something. Ava needed space. Time. Maybe the chance to slap him across the face. How could one man twist up her insides so much while simultaneously ripping out her heart? Silly her for assuming their passionate night meant more than it did. They'd had sex. That was it. Plenty of people had one-night-stands. And now it was time to move on.

Chapter 5

Sam swiped his badge and moved into the secure area of Shadow Security Headquarters Wednesday morning, his teammates close behind him. They were briefing with Jett Hutchinson, their boss and the head of Shadow Security, preparing to move out on a mission that night. Jett came striding out of his office, his face tense, and nodded at the rest of the team as he hustled down the hall.

"He looks pissed," Gray Pierce said, his eyes narrowing as Jett ducked into the conference room ahead of the rest of them.

"Yep," Sam said, offering no further comment.

"What's with you?" Nick Dowd asked, slugging Sam in the shoulder. They entered the meeting space as Jett was already pulling up slides on the laptop at the front of the room.

"Huh? Nothing. Just thinking," Sam muttered.

Luke flashed him a knowing look, amused and

slightly smug. Of course, he was. His girlfriend had just moved in with him and life was fucking spectacular. Sam hadn't exactly been looking for a serious relationship in the past, but he'd have to be blind to miss how happy his teammates were with their women. A lot had happened over the past year. Ford Anderson was engaged to Clara, the receptionist at Shadow Security. She and her young daughter had moved in with him, and their wedding was next month. Jett and his fiancée Anna had just welcomed their first baby. Anna had been helping to run the administrative side of things in the office but was now on maternity leave—most likely permanently, if Jett had his way.

Sam recalled how sick Anna had been—morning sickness to the extreme or something. Jett's normally protective streak had been amplified to the max. He'd always doted on Anna, but he'd been frantic during her pregnancy. Jett had chilled out slightly after she'd given birth but checked his phone more often than usual to make sure she and their baby were okay.

It was cute, really. Their gruff boss smitten over his woman and child.

Sam shook his head. Everything felt different around here. He wouldn't be surprised if Luke popped the question to Wren someday. Ava couldn't exactly avoid him if their best friends got married, could she?

Shit.

Seeing her in Mexico last month had been like a punch to the gut. When he'd spotted her in the lobby, it was like something out of a movie. Time stopped. His vision had tunneled. And his entire world had been tilted on its axis. His complete focus had been

SAM

on her as she'd walked in—the look of shock on her face, the silky strawberry-blonde hair that had tickled his thighs, those creamy breasts that he'd—hell. He let out a choked sound. Ava had been on his mind since the moment she'd reappeared in his life, and wasn't that just fucking fantastic.

There were other women. Millions of people in New York. But none of them were her.

Nick crossed his arms, leaning back in his chair as Jett muttered a curse. The other guys were grabbing seats as well, and Sam yanked back a chair at the long conference table, sitting down with a thump. Maybe this op would get his mind off the past weekend and Ava's hurt gaze. Her anger he could handle, but that look of devastation? It was a damn punch to the gut.

"Wedding planning stressing you out?" Nick joked as Jett uncharacteristically knocked over a stack of papers after he'd pulled up the slides for their briefing.

Jett flashed him a look, leaning down to snatch everything off the floor. "I just got off the phone with Anna a few minutes ago. She had a doctor appointment—a standard checkup or whatnot. Anna assured me it was no big deal, so I didn't go."

"Everything okay?" Sam asked, sitting up straighter and leaning forward.

"She's pregnant."

A beat passed. "What?" Sam said, his gaze narrowing.

"Anna's pregnant again. They were running some routine labs and did a pregnancy test. It came back positive. They did bloodwork and an early ultrasound, and she's exactly six weeks along."

The room was silent for a beat before filling with

loud conversation, the men rising from their seats and clapping him on the back, offering their congratulations. "Hot damn!" Nick whooped as he shook Jett's hand. "Your boys are some real swimmers."

The men burst into laughter, Sam trying to cover his snickering as Jett leveled Nick with another look. "It's a blessing, but I'm worried about my fiancée," he ground out. "Anna's last pregnancy wasn't easy, and this happened sooner than expected."

"She'll be fine, boss," Gray said, crossing his arms from where he'd remained seated at the conference table, watching the commotion in the room. "I'm not much into kids, but Anna's a natural. She's incredible with your little guy. And she handled the morning sickness the first time. I think she was calmer than you. Wasn't she just gushing a couple of weeks ago how she wanted a houseful of kids?"

"And I can't deny her anything," Jett said, his lips quirking as he shook his head.

"No one would blame you for not being able to keep your hands off her," Nick said, waggling his eyebrows. "She's a beautiful woman."

"Easy," Sam muttered, shaking his head as Jett shot Nick another look. No doubt any living and breathing man would agree that Anna was gorgeous, but she was their boss's fiancée. Anna wasn't Sam's type, anyway. She was high-maintenance, impulsive, and went over-the-top with everything she did. Ava was headstrong and opinionated like Anna but somehow more laid back and carefree about life. A free-spirit. An artist. And so fucking pretty it made his chest hurt.

"Here I thought you were worked up about the

mission," Ford said, returning to his chair at the table after congratulating Jett.

"Not this time," Jett replied. "Just a curveball I wasn't expecting. The op should be easy in and easy out, which brings us around to the actual purpose of this briefing."

The rest of the men grabbed their seats as Jett clicked on the first slide, nodding at Luke in the back of the room to dim the lights.

"You'll be flying into Syria to take out an HVT," Jett said. "Abou El Din is the head of the Syrian branch of ISIS, with ties to the group's branches in other parts of the Middle East and North Africa. El Din was behind the massive explosion in the Syrian market last week that killed seventy-three victims and injured countless others. Intelligence assessments indicate that he's attempting to smuggle weapons out of the country and into the U.S., in preparations for an attack here.

Killing El Din will temporarily cripple the operation as various subordinates try to take over the group. The Pentagon has asked us to move in given raw intelligence on his current location. U.S. government officials are currently in talks with the Syrians and don't want to jeopardize their tenuous agreement by sending in the military. It's a tricky balance. Although the Syrian government would love to cut the head off the snake, so to speak, they don't want further retaliation in their own country."

"So it's entirely off the books," Gray confirmed.

"Affirmative. The U.S. government will not be stepping in should anything go wrong. We're on our own. Abou El Din will be mysteriously taken out, presumably by his own subordinates struggling to gain power as far as the rest of the world is concerned."

"Well hell," Sam muttered. "Nothing like stirring up a little shit."

"You said he has ties to other branches of ISIS. Are they involved in the weapons smuggling operation?" Luke asked.

"Yes. ISIS has a stronghold in the Middle East but is pushing to get these weapons to others in their terror network. They're looking to smuggle munitions across the Mediterranean Sea to Cairo, according to signals intelligence."

Sam's ears perked up. "Cairo?" He exchanged a glance with Luke, who clenched his fist.

Jett nodded. "There's an Egyptian branch of ISIS that would be extremely happy to acquire these weapons. SIGINT indicates that they're looking for weak spots, determined to find ways to smuggle weapons into the United States. El Din is more than happy to work with them, given their common goal of harming Americans and others in the Western World. Assassinating the Syrian ISIS leader will stall them, delaying the movement of the munitions to Egypt as they scramble for a new leader.

The group has access to military grade weapons, rocket launchers, and explosives. Analysts assess that the explosives material is what they're trying to smuggle into the country. The U.S. military is making plans to move in to Syria after talks between U.S. officials and their Syrian counterparts have been completed. Current intelligence pinpoints El Din at a specific location for the next several days. We don't have time to waste. Moving in immediately is imperative, and until these talks are completed, the

U.S. military cannot be involved. That doesn't stop us from taking action as our job will be entirely off the books. Abou El Din is an arrogant man who doesn't expect the Syrian Government to act or allow U.S. forces to intervene. He believes he is safe in his own country. You'll fly in, eliminate the target, and immediately fly back out. The struggle for power that ensues will give us enough time to stop the movement of the weapons. Let's go over the specifics."

***

An hour later, the men were hustling out of the conference room. Jett was already on the phone with Anna, and the others were discussing details for their mission, making preparations to move out that evening.

"You okay, man?" Luke asked as he caught up to Sam in the hallway.

Sam glanced back over his shoulder, eyeing his teammate. "Of course. Just heading down to the armory to start gathering weapons and supplies."

"Don't bullshit me."

"Cairo's dangerous," Sam said, not even bothering to mention Ava. They both knew who he was talking about—why he was concerned. "It burns me up that she's going there for the summer and potentially putting herself in danger, not that she cares what I think."

"It wasn't my idea to leave you and Ava alone the other day," Luke said in a low voice. "Wren thought you needed to talk."

Sam raised an eyebrow. "In the middle of moving

out of her apartment? Seems like it wasn't really the time or place to hope to get back in Ava's good graces."

Luke shrugged. "Yeah, well, Ava's been pissed at you for a while."

"No shit."

His friend's laughter filled the stairwell as they quietly moved down to the basement of headquarters. "Wren thought if you were stuck together, you'd talk things through. Mexico was a stressful situation, but we've been back for a month. Just try to get along. Wren's worried we can't all hang out together because Ava's so pissed at you. It was kind of a dick move, man. Not responding to her texts and blowing her off like that was harsh."

Sam muttered a curse. "The fuck? You think I don't know that? We were gone for weeks on our op. I had to get my head on straight and put Paris behind me. After that? I moved on. Too much time had passed, and I thought it was for the best."

"Yeah, sure. You moved on. That's just what it looked like when you ran into her again down in Mexico."

"Asshole," Sam muttered.

"I just want Wren to be happy," Luke admitted. "She went through hell with her sister's kidnaping. It would be easier if her best friend and boyfriend's friends got along. You don't have to marry the girl, just apologize and get her to stop looking like she's ready to murder you at the first chance."

"I wouldn't put it past her," Sam ground out. "Doesn't really matter anyway. She's leaving, remember? Taking that sculpture commission in Egypt. Honestly, it sounds shady as fuck. Why the

SAM

hell can't she work in her studio space here? Inspiration, my ass. I think she's just looking for a reason to get out of here."

"Is she? You met her in Paris. She was traveling around Europe then and flew down to Mexico at a moment's notice to help Wren. She's adventurous—just right for a guy like you."

Sam scrubbed a hand over his face, letting out a groan. "Now you're trying to set us up? Even if I hadn't botched up a chance with her, she's leaving. Once again, the timing is wrong. It just wasn't meant to be, buddy."

They swiped their badges and moved into the secure armory, Luke flashing him a pointed look. "Long before I actually met Ava, you'd talk about the girl you met in Paris. The one who got away. Best sex of your life, was it? The night you'll never forget?"

"It was a vacation fling," Sam said, grinding his teeth. "A one-night-stand. It didn't mean a damn thing."

"Sure. That's why you're both always going at it. You were goading her down in Mexico, and don't even try to deny it. Maybe you need to bang her again to get her out of your system."

"Don't talk about her that way," Sam seethed, shooting Luke a look that could kill.

Luke smirked, looking far too pleased with himself. "Don't care about her, huh? Keep telling yourself that."

Sam shook his head and stormed across the room, yanking open one of the storage lockers. "I don't have time to talk about this right now. I've got a job to focus on. A mission. Maybe Ava Kincaid and I just weren't meant to be."

Chapter 6

"My God, it is gorgeous out here," Ava admitted Friday night, looking up at the stars from Luke and Wren's backyard. She smiled as the hammock she was stretched out in swayed back and forth in the gentle breeze, the softness of the night surrounding her. "It's nothing like down in the city. I bet you can see every star from here."

"You can see a lot of them. Luke said this always felt like home," Wren said wistfully. "He traveled extensively in the military but couldn't say no when Jett offered him a job in upstate New York. I totally get it. It's peaceful here in a way Manhattan never is."

"Do you miss it?" Ava asked, glancing over at her best friend, who was currently sprawled out on a chaise lounge, wearing one of Luke's sweatshirts.

"Sometimes I miss the hustle and bustle of Manhattan," Wren admitted. "The energy and excitement. I like that I'm still close enough to get into the city when I want. I can write from anywhere though, do phone interviews, and easily commute if I need to meet with a source."

Ava shot her friend a curious glance. "Are you happy here?"

Wren grinned. "Absolutely. I wouldn't change moving in with Luke for anything. I felt uncomfortable in my studio apartment anyway after we got back from Mexico. Now I know why, what with that crazy Marine who was after me. This feels right, though—good. I know we haven't been together long, but I love living with him. I kind of jumped headfirst into this relationship, but we both just knew it was right. Someday, Luke and I will get married and have kids, and I definitely want a house and a yard. I don't want to raise children in the city. Besides, my studio would've been cramped even with just the two of us. I love it here."

"Well, damn," Ava said, gently pushing herself in the hammock with one bare foot on the ground. "You're on your way to the whole American dream—house, future kids. Pretty soon Luke will put up the white picket fence and all."

"Ha ha. We're not in a rush to have children, but if it happens? I'm ready for it."

"Please at least let me throw you a wild bachelorette party before you completely settle down and have kids. I want to serve some of those penis-shaped cookies and get those straws shaped like dicks. Oh, I could sculpt a phallic-shaped cake, too. I'm an artist, not a pastry chef, but I could make it work."

Wren couldn't contain her laughter. "And who would be the model for such a masterpiece?"

"Well, I have seen the perfect dick—too bad the

man himself was a total ass."

"Oh really?" Wren asked, suddenly seeming more interested. "And would this guy have a name that starts with 'S' and ends with 'am'?"

"You'll never know," Ava teased. "But seriously, here you're talking about your entire future, and I'm still aimlessly traveling around the world."

"Not aimlessly," Wren stressed. "Girl, you're an amazing artist. You've got an incredible opportunity this summer. And those paintings you sent me pictures of earlier this week? Incredible. I bet one day you'll be selling them for a million bucks and have large gallery openings all over the world in your name. You'll leave us peons in the dust."

Ava couldn't help laughing. "I'm happy with the way my sales are going, but I don't know. Art and travel have always been my jam, but lately it kind of feels like something is missing. That's partly why I took the job in Egypt. I felt like I needed to do something bigger—something more." She stared up at the sky, waiting as her friend mulled that over.

"Well, I'm proud of you. Not everyone is gutsy enough to pack up and travel to a foreign country alone like that."

"When have I not been gutsy?" Ava asked. "That's like my superpower and weakness. I jump right into things whether it'll hurt or not."

"Point taken. It's just—who knows? Maybe this will open up some new opportunities for you. You're so talented, Ava. Goodness knows that I can write, but that's it. I couldn't paint a stick figure."

"Oh, stop," Ava said, laughing. "You absolutely could paint a stick figure, girlfriend."

"Exactly," Wren muttered. "That's not a talent."

SAM

"Where's the wine?" Ava giggled. "I think I need another glass."

"Coming right up," Wren joked as she stood and padded barefoot across the patio. Wren picked up the second bottle of wine from the end table and popped the cork, pouring the Cabernet into their empty glasses.

"When do you think the guys will be back?" Ava asked lightly.

Wren shot her a look. "I'm not sure. Luke can't ever tell me about their missions—except when I crashed their op in Mexico, that is. He said this was pretty straight forward, whatever that means. I know when they were looking for Lily, they were still gathering intel. It sounds like with this mission, they were moving in to do whatever they do."

"It's dangerous," Ava said unnecessarily.

"Yep," Wren agreed, setting the bottle of red back on the table and bringing a glass to Ava. "I try not to think about it too much. Luke and his friends are good at what they do—the best. My worrying won't change anything."

"They were Special Forces, right? When they were in the military?"

"Yeah, they were. I think they basically do the same things now, except it's off the books. Their missions are shorter, too. It's not like they deploy for a year somewhere. It's dangerous as hell, but who am I to say anything? They rushed down to rescue Lily, and I'll be eternally grateful for that. If they're helping other people and doing good in the world, they're heroes in my book. I'd never be brave enough to do what they do, but those guys were cut out for jobs like this."

"They'll be fine," Ava said confidently. "They were together for years, right? I'm sure this is a piece of cake for them." She took a sip of her wine, looking up at the stars again. Was Sam somewhere on the other side of the world, looking at the same sky? Not that it mattered. She wouldn't wish harm to him, but she didn't need to waste time thinking about him either.

"So what day are you heading to Egypt?" Wren asked. "Did they book your flights?"

"I'm leaving in two weeks. It's perfect timing, actually. I've got an art show next weekend at a small gallery in Manhattan. You should totally come, by the way. You and Luke. Hopefully I can sell some pieces there, but I told the gallery owner that I'll be traveling over the summer. I'll probably do another show later in the fall if this one is successful. I'll be busy with my sculptures of course while I'm in Cairo but will bring my sketchbooks. I'd love to paint some of the pyramids and ancient ruins if I have enough time to travel on the weekends Maybe that could be the theme for my next showing," she said with a shrug.

"I'm going to miss you this summer," Wren admitted.

"Oh, you will not," Ava chastised. "You'll be jumping your man when he walks in the front door, having crazy sex every night." Wren flushed, causing Ava to laugh. "Please, girl. Like I didn't hear his comments about your sexy lingerie when we were packing up your place? The man is smitten, and good for you. I can tell you're head over heels in love with him, too. You'll get to play house with your new boyfriend, starting your lives together, and I'll live my best life as a single artist traveling abroad. No one-night-stands this time, though," she added, shuddering. Ava lifted her wine glass into the air, grinning. "To the best summer of our lives!"

Wren leaned over, clinking her glass against Ava's. "To new beginnings," she said, taking a sip of her wine. "And the best summer ever."

"Now you're talking," Ava said with a wink.

Chapter 7

Sam scrubbed a hand over his jaw and climbed out of Luke's SUV, feeling the ache in his muscles from sleeping in a tent on the hard ground over the past week. It was a far cry from their stint to Mexico where they'd had hotel rooms but was on par with his Army days. Nothing like roughing it to make you appreciate your own bed. Not that he had anyone to share it with.

"Thanks for the ride, man," Sam said, reaching back in to grab his duffle bag.

"Anytime," Luke replied. "It's good to be back."

Gray hopped out of the backseat, calling out thanks as he slammed the door and strode across the parking lot of Shadow Security Headquarters toward his large pick-up truck. He tossed his gear in the back and then climbed into the driver's seat, not bothering to look back.

Luke cocked his head in the direction their buddy

SAM

had gone. "What's his deal?"

Sam lifted a shoulder. "Dunno. He's always been reserved about some things, but it's been even more noticeable since we got out of the service. Maybe he's got a secret woman he's rushing home to," Sam joked.

"Doubt it."

"Yeah, well, the hell if I know. Gray will talk when he's ready. We've all got our own demons to deal with." Sam eyed Luke, his hand resting on the top of the door before he headed to his own truck. "You talk with Wren yet? I'm assuming it was hard to leave for a week after you just moved her in to your place."

Luke smiled at the mention of his girlfriend. "Yep. The timing sucked, but it's not like we deploy for months on end like we did in the Army. I texted her from the airport, and she was ecstatic that we're back. She sent me messages every day while we were gone," Luke added with a chuckle. "Wren said she knew I probably couldn't see them but missed me."

Sam nodded once, his lips quirking. Ava had tried that. Sort of. It wasn't the same thing, but she'd been thinking about him enough to shoot him a few texts during her travels last year, and he'd blown her off, ruining any chance he might've had. "I guess you don't know if Ava's left yet."

Luke looked surprised for a beat. "Think she's got another week here," Luke told him. "She's got some big art show in the city this weekend. Wren hoped I'd be back in time to go with her. You should come," he added, looking thoughtful.

"Nah. Don't want to mess up that night for her. An art show sounds like a big deal," he added. "When we were moving Wren out of her place, I saw that amazing painting on the wall. It shocked the hell out of me when Wren said Ava had painted it. I knew she was an artist, but damn. I don't have any sort of talent like that," he said, shaking his head.

"Neither do most of us," Luke said wryly. "Ava's one of a kind. But I don't know…taking out terrorists has its place in the world."

Sam chuffed out a laugh despite himself. "That's dark, dude. True, but fucking dark."

Luke nodded, pressing his lips together. They both knew what he wasn't saying. None of them took death lightly. If taking out dangerous men meant saving the lives of hundreds or thousands of others, it was tough to feel the guilt though. They'd seen all sorts of evil throughout the world, and ridding mankind of the worst of humanity wasn't something he'd ever feel remorse for. They helped more than hurt people, and that was why the men had all joined the Shadow Ops Team. They served a purpose in this world, even if most civilians would never know a thing about it.

"It's the goddamn truth," Luke said. "But listen, I still think you should come to the art show with us. Wren wants to have a little celebration. It's a big deal for Ava, so it'll be kind of a celebratory party and going away affair."

"I don't think she wants to see me."

Luke raised his eyebrows. "You sure about that? Because sometimes I think it's like that quote—the lady doth protest too much."

Sam burst into laughter. "Is that Shakespeare? Shit, man, this is too deep for me. Say hi to Wren," he added, stepping back to close the door.

"Think about it!" Luke called out.

SAM

The door slammed shut, and Sam shook his head as he moved away in the dark, his duffle bag gripped in his hand. Jett had gotten some other employees to offload the gear from the plane and get everything put away back at headquarters. His job was done for now. They'd debrief tomorrow but had gotten their man. Taking out El Din would slow down the Syrian branch of ISIS, but it wouldn't stop them. Not by a long shot. He just hoped the ramifications of what they'd accomplished and any retaliation on the part of the terror network wouldn't trickle down to Cairo while Ava was there.

Sam clicked the remote and tossed his duffle bag into his truck, climbing in before shutting the door. He leaned back in the driver's seat, briefly closing his eyes. Damn he was tired. The type of tired you felt deep in your bones—not just exhaustion, but physical weariness. He looked down at his phone with a deep sigh, knowing there wasn't a chance in hell Ava had texted him. That ship had sailed.

And if it felt just a little bit lonely heading down the winding, wooded road leading away from headquarters in the middle of the night, then so be it. Sam was just fine on his own.

***

"Look at you princess, looking all pretty for me."

Ava smiled and slowly turned around, showing off her toned ass in a sexy thong. Her hands covered her bare breasts, barely concealing her nipples, and Sam moved closer, wanting to touch. Taste. Needing to see all of her.

"Do you want me, Sam?" Ava licked her lips, a smile playing about on her lips.

Sam reached out, wanting to touch some of that soft skin, feel those smooth curves. Ava was so close. So goddamn tempting. "Ava," he ground out. Her floral scent teased him, reminding him of that endless Paris night, of how sweet she tasted.

"Touch me, Sam. I want you to—"

Sam jolted in his sleep, the buzzing of the phone on his nightstand jarring him from his erotic dream. He blinked groggily, his cock stiff and aching, pushing against the boxer briefs he hadn't bothered to remove last night. Pre-come leaked from the head of his cock as it strained to get free, and he felt like he was ready to explode.

It had been a goddamn dream, but it had felt so fucking real. She'd been right there, close enough to—

Groaning, he reached over and fumbled with his phone as it buzzed again. Adrenaline coursed through his veins, and he willed his body to calm down. He blinked at the screen. Luke. Why the hell was his buddy calling him so early? Wait. What time was it?

"Yeah?" he asked as he swiped the screen.

"Good morning to you, too, sunshine," Luke quipped.

"Is there a reason you're calling me so early?"

"It's not early. You're late. Boss wants to meet in thirty."

Sam rubbed his eyes, looking at the clock on his nightstand. "Shit. I crashed after I got home and forgot to set my alarm. Jesus. I haven't done that in—ever."

"Briefing's at oh-nine-hundred. And I figured," Luke said with a low chuckle. "It's not like you to be late. See you when you get here."

SAM

Sam muttered a curse as he ended the call, tossing the phone back down. "Fuck my life," he said, clamping one big hand down over his eyes. His other moved to his cock, gripping it firmly through his boxer briefs. He needed to lose the hard-on and get ready. Now he had visions of Ava's luscious body dancing through his mind. He'd gone nearly a year without letting himself think of her, and then in Mexico, it had all come crashing down.

Losing the boxers, Sam stroked himself, twisting his hand as he reached the head of his engorged shaft. What he needed was Ava—her smart mouth and full lips. The swipes of her tongue. The way she'd sucked him off in the shower that morning, eagerly taking all of him. He twisted his hand again, moving faster, and exploded, unable to stop the streams of come spurting from his dick.

"God damn you, woman," he muttered, wiping himself off with his boxers before rising and stalking toward the bathroom. He tossed the discarded clothing into the hamper, remembering that his other dirty clothes were still stuffed in his duffle bag. It was just his luck that Ava was now tempting him in his dreams. Even his unconscious self wanted her. He turned on the spray in his shower, his stiff muscles relaxing a minute later as he stepped under the hot water. The ibuprofen he'd taken last night had dulled the stiffness in his back, but it would be a couple of days before he felt one hundred percent again.

Sam leaned his head against the cool tiles, letting the hot water wash over him. He wasn't as young as he used to be, but at thirty-four, he wasn't that damn old either. Ava was younger than him, probably in her late twenties. He let out a resigned sigh. He needed to get a move-on to make it to headquarters for their briefing. He didn't need to spend his morning dwelling on the what-ifs. Their op had gone smoothly, and no doubt the government would be pleased that the Shadow Ops Team had completed another successful mission. His teammates were happy to get home to their women.

And Sam? He was still fucking alone and just fine with that.

He quickly soaped up his body, his thoughts churning. Uneasiness washed over him as he recalled the anger in Abou El Din's eyes, the hatred he and his subordinates had for the Western World. The Shadow Ops Team might've taken out the leader of the Syrian branch of ISIS, but the terror network was still alive and well, intent on harming innocent civilians. Ava was still headed to a dangerous place, where she'd be a single woman living alone.

"Mother-fucker," he muttered. She might hate him, but he needed to talk to her before she left. He didn't want to scare her, but she was free-spirited and trusting. She needed to at least understand the potential dangers. Maybe he would go to that art show. He'd offer his assistance if she needed something while in Cairo for the summer. Let her know they had contacts all over the world. Ava would be fine, but he'd feel better after he spoke with her nonetheless.

Chapter 8

Ava moved around the swanky art gallery on Saturday evening in her sky-high heels and sleek strapless dress, a glass of champagne in one hand. She'd curled her long hair so it bounced around her cleavage as she walked and had done her make-up just so: dark red lipstick that didn't clash with her strawberry-blonde locks, a smokey eye, and tons of mascara since her eyelashes were almost nonexistent.

"Oh, this one is breathtaking!" a woman declared, staring at the painting that featured an elegant group of ballerinas posing at a barre.

"Simply stunning," another agreed. "Look at the lines and how graceful their hands are. The detail is amazing."

Ava smiled and continued walking, listening to snippets of conversations. People were still arriving, and the gallery owner was planning to introduce her to the guests soon, after welcoming everyone to the showing. Ava's gaze swept the space as she paused, feeling content. A few of her friends had already arrived as well as other artists she knew who'd come to celebrate and support her. Some wealthy patrons of the gallery had just walked in, and Ava recognized them from a fellow artist's showing in the spring. A Middle Eastern man in the corner caught her attention, standing alone and talking on a cell phone. She didn't recognize him, but New York was a huge place. She could've seen him every day and had no idea thanks to the large population. He frowned and continued speaking into his phone before moving toward the doors.

As she watched him leave, she grinned, spotting Wren and Luke coming inside. "You made it!" Ava gushed, rushing over to see them. "I'm so happy you could come."

Wren wrapped her in a big hug and then handed her a bouquet of flowers. "I didn't know what was appropriate for a showing like this. I'm so excited for you, hun! Congratulations." Her gaze briefly swept the gallery. "Wow. This is amazing."

"Thank you. And the flowers are gorgeous," Ava said, taking the sleek calla lilies from her friend.

"This is incredible," Luke agreed. "I know nothing about art, but you're clearly quite talented. Looks like a good turnout, too," he added as more people came in the front doors.

"I'm thrilled so many people are here," Ava admitted. "I was a little nervous with this being my first solo show. What if no one showed up? I've been blasting social medial channels all week trying to get the word out."

"You're cutting it kind of close to your trip," Wren

said with a grin. "If I was leaving for the summer in a week's time, I'd be frantically packing, not walking around looking all fancy with a glass of champagne in one hand."

One of the gallery assistants walked over, offering to take the flowers from Ava and giving her a brief update on the timeline for the evening.

"You'd really pack a week early?" Ava joked, looking back at her friend. "You know I'll be packing everything the night before. I'll even check a suitcase this time since I'll be there so long. I'll be carrying on my art supplies, of course. I don't want to risk losing them."

"They're not supplying you with materials?" Luke asked, crinkling his brow.

"Oh, they are for the sculptures," Ava clarified. "But I travel with my own brushes and charcoals to sketch. You never know when inspiration will strike. I'll pick up some paints in Cairo since I don't need them exploding in my suitcase or something."

"Well, you are an artist," Wren pointed out. "What's a little paint on your clothes?"

"Ha ha. Even I have my limits."

"Where do you paint when you're here in the city?" Luke asked. "In your apartment?"

"I rent a commercial studio space with some other artists. I do some painting at home but work in other mediums and need a larger room, like with some of the bigger sculptures I've done. Gotta let my creativity flow, you know?"

"Gotcha," Luke said. "And that's primarily what you'll be doing this summer? Sculptures?"

"There aren't any sculptures here today," Wren told him, realizing his confusion. "This is Ava's collection of paintings depicting life in New York—a glimpse into the life of the typical and atypical New Yorker."

"You read the material for the show," Ava said.

"Of course. I'm a reporter. You know I read every bit of info I can get my hands on."

"So, what type of sculptures will you work on over the summer?" Luke asked.

"It will mostly be large pieces for a wealthy client there. Upon completion, they'll be displayed in the lobby of a prominent building in Cairo. They need something bold and unique. They did seem interested in some smaller works, too. By coincidence, the man who commissioned the pieces has family here in New York. He mentioned some smaller-scale sculptures he'd like me to do. If I end up making those, I might travel back with them myself. He thought it'd be a nice touch if I hand-delivered them, so to speak."

"Huh." Luke said, looking perplexed.

Wren was watching the front door and then looked back to Ava, having missed most of the conversation. "That reminds me, let's chat a minute," she said, grabbing Ava's arm and dragging her aside as she called back to Luke to grab them some drinks.

"What's wrong?" Ava asked, taking a quick sip of her champagne. The bubbles tingled on her tongue, and for a flash, she was back at the hotel room in Paris—naked in bed with Sam, sipping champagne with him. She steeled herself, shaking her head. It was one night. One. Night. It was nothing.

"Sam's coming tonight," Wren said, and Ava nearly spit out her drink.

"What?"

"I sort of told him about the show," Wren rushed

SAM

on. "I know you're pissed at him, but he's apologized several times for blowing you off. I know he regrets it, and Luke is one of his best friends. Can we put the past in the past? Move forward? You're leaving soon, but when you get back, we'll all be together sometimes. I want to be able to have parties where Luke and I can invite all of our friends. If Sam's there, I don't want you to make some excuse to not come."

"Wren," Ava said, rolling her eyes. "I don't need to make up an excuse. He gave me as good a reason as any to dislike him with the shit way he acted. Sam's the type of guy who only thinks with his dick. Inviting him to my big opening was a bad idea."

"I'm sorry for not telling you sooner, but it'll be fine. He'll stay out of your way. I think he was curious about your artwork. Plus, we're celebrating afterwards, remember? There will be lots of people around to act as a buffer at the party. You barely even need to talk to him—just coexist in the same room together."

"Yeah, right," Ava muttered. "Most men have no interest in talking, but Sam seems perfectly happy bringing up Paris whenever he can."

"He's sorry. I thought he was a jerk, too, but I guess it was a really stressful situation for them. Luke can't tell me about their missions, but I know they're hardcore. They need to be 'in the zone,' so to speak. I think he really feels bad about it."

"He only feels bad because he saw me again," Ava pointed out. "Sam wasn't exactly going out of his way to track me down or apologize. It's been a year."

"There you are," the gallery director said, rushing over to Ava and effectively ending the conversation. "I'm planning to welcome everyone to the event and want to introduce you to the guests in a couple of minutes. Are you ready for your big debut? We're thrilled to showcase your pieces here this evening."

"But of course I'm ready," Ava said, laughing as she downed the rest of her champagne, excitement bubbling within her. She set the empty glass on the tray of a passing waiter and said goodbye to Wren, moving with the director to the front of the room. She waved at a group of her artist friends, grinning as one of them gave her the thumbs-up, and then took a deep breath as the gallery director stepped up to the microphone. This was it—her first solo showing. Her work had been featured in multiple art shows over the years, but this was her first time headlining in an art gallery. It might be small, but it was a start. The opportunity was incredible, and she knew she'd remember this night for the rest of her life.

The group gathered began to hush as they realized the evening was officially about to begin.

Ava beamed as the woman welcomed the guests, her eyes scanning the room. Wren had snuggled back up next to Luke, and some of her friends were clustered together, smiling at her, glasses of champagne in their hands. The waiters carrying silver trays of appetizers were at the sides of the room, waiting to continue when the speech was over.

"Ava Kincaid is no stranger to the art world. Her pieces on New York are showcased here tonight, and we look forward to many opportunities in the future to work together again. Without further ado, I'd like to introduce you to the artist herself—Ms. Ava Kincaid!"

She stepped up to the microphone, taking in the crowd of people. It was the perfect evening—art, cocktails and champagne, appetizers, and her closest friends. Her heart pounded with excitement and anticipation. She'd worked so hard for this, had put her heart and soul into her paintings, and her dreams of succeeding in the art world were finally becoming reality.

"Thank you for coming tonight," she said.

The door to the gallery opened, and for a split-second, her gaze shifted, the rest of the crowd disappearing into the background. Warmth washed over her skin, pooling in her veins, and a different type of excitement wove through her. Ava needed to continue speaking, to welcome the guests to her show. Instead, her breath caught as Sam's piercing gaze met hers.

Chapter 9

Sam stilled after he'd walked through the gallery doors, spotting Ava standing there shining in the spotlight. Glossy, strawberry-blonde hair spilled down her shoulders, brushing against her creamy cleavage. A well-fitting dress hugged her curves and hit at midthigh, showing off toned, sexy legs. Strappy, high-heeled sandals gave her a couple of extra inches, and for a flash, he imagined her wearing those and nothing else.

Ava looked like a goddess. Ethereal. Confident. Beaming.

He caught the surprise on her face as he walked in, and she quickly schooled her expression. Even from across the room he could see the way her breath hitched, her breasts rising and pushing against the tight dress.

He affected her, whether she'd admit as much or not. Desire coiled within him. Despite the time and

SAM

space between them, he loved knowing she hadn't forgotten either.

Sam stayed where he was in the background, and he could tell she was a touch nervous. She was still smiling, her cheeks flushed, but her gaze flickered to him only once more before she proceeded to look at anyone and everyone else.

Sam remembered the pretty flush that had spread over her ivory skin as he'd thoroughly pleasured her. Made her cry out his name and come undone at his touch.

She turned to her right, the waves in her silky hair dancing around her breasts with the movement. Every man in the room was staring at her, and he felt a possessiveness rising within him. He had no claim on her, no right to want her so badly, but that didn't stop the caveman inside him demanding to make her his and his alone.

"I'm thrilled you're all here tonight," Ava said, looking back at the crowd. "Art is my passion—my reason and purpose. I've traveled the world with my sketchbooks, but no place is like New York. These pieces showcase life in the city, true New Yorkers, and I hope you'll appreciate them as much as I do. I tried to capture the big and small—all the moments. I'll be traveling more this summer for work, but you can follow along on social media to see my work. Hopefully we'll meet here again in the fall," she said, winking at the gallery director as the audience chuckled. "And now—enjoy your evening! I'm here to answer any questions or talk about the art world in general. Thank you again for coming."

Sam was moving without thought as she stepped away from the microphone. Stay in the background be dammed. He'd congratulate her—and glare at any man who dared get too close.

The gallery door opened behind him, and Sam hastened a glance back to see a Middle Eastern man step in. He wasn't looking at any of the artwork but moved through the crowd, pulling out his cell phone to snap a few pictures. Sam felt his hackles rising. No one else seemed to be photographing the evening's guests. Everyone else was focused on the art work and Ava.

Luke caught his gaze, and Sam nodded once, cocking his head toward the guy. Luke moved toward the man, who quickly slid his phone into his pocket as he saw Luke coming and made a hasty exit. Luke followed him to the door, stepping outside.

Sam stepped in front of the gallery owner as she passed by. "Who was that man taking photos? He came in a minute ago and walked through the crowd."

"The photojournalist?" she asked in confusion.

Sam followed her gaze to another man who was adjusting the settings on a professional camera. "No. Some guy just popped in with a cell phone. He snapped pictures of the crowd and Ava and then walked back out."

The gallery owner didn't look concerned. "It's probably just a college kid. They like to post pictures on social media of events around the city. We've been publicizing this."

Sam clenched his jaw. "No. This guy was older, maybe in his late-thirties."

"Was he causing problems?" she asked, suddenly looking nonplussed. "Where is he now?"

"He already left."

The gallery director's gaze slid to the door as Luke

SAM

walked back in, Wren moving to his side. "Well, it's not an invitation-only event. We're always looking to get word out about our artists and showings. If someone wants to post photos of the gallery's events online, I'm not opposed to it. We can use the publicity. Let me know if you see him again."

"Will do," Sam said with a frown. The woman hurried off, snagging a glass of champagne and hurrying toward an older couple. No doubt she was anxious to make a few sales this evening. Ava's paintings were incredible, but he knew it was about the money as much as the art. This was a business, and the gallery owner needed to pay her rent just like everyone else.

Sam stalked toward Ava, hearing her laughter from across the room. She truly was in her element, talking with guests and gesturing toward one wall filled with her art. Her slender hand pointed at one painting in particular, and he recalled the feeling of her nails raking down his back, her legs wrapped tightly around him.

She was leaving in seven days, and if he knew what was good for him, he'd turn around and walk the other way.

Sam moved closer.

"Ava," he ground out.

She turned to look up at him, her lips thinning as she pressed them together. The guests were still chatting, but her blue eyes were focused only on Sam as she took a step toward him. Her hips shifted with the movement, and his eyes were briefly drawn to her shapely legs and sexy heels. Ava was a vixen. A goddess. The woman had him by the balls and didn't even know it. "Sam," she said cooly, her voice a contrast to the fire in her eyes. "I didn't expect to see you here tonight. I wouldn't think art shows would be of much interest to you."

He raised his eyebrows. "I followed you all over Paris, princess. I seem to remember visiting multiple galleries that day." His gaze briefly flicked around the room. "I have to admit, this is incredible. Right on par with the paintings we saw in Paris together. You're extremely talented."

Ava crossed her arms, which did nothing but draw his gaze toward her cleavage. Damn. The woman had pretty breasts. "Huh. Well, the past is in the past," Ava said. "Thanks for coming."

Sam grabbed her elbow before she could completely turn away. Her skin was so damn soft and smooth. Warm. He could easily see over her shoulder as he towered above her, looking down at the tops of her full breasts. If he buried his face in that silkiness, he knew he'd be surrounded by her floral scent. He could make it good for her. Kiss his way down her body and listen to her soft cries. Taste her ripe pussy. Sam knew exactly how to make her writhe and moan—and how it felt to sink balls deep inside of her.

She stilled, her breath catching. She looked straight ahead but hadn't yanked her arm away. "Yes, Sam? Was there something else you needed to say?"

Ava finally pulled her arm from his grip but turned to look at him, those blue eyes all too knowing. Everything about Ava appealed to him. She was sexy, sassy, and talented as hell. Smart. Adventurous. And she didn't take his shit either, which he appreciated. Ava was a woman who would tell it like it is, always keeping him on his toes. Just being around her made

SAM

life more exciting, and that said a lot for a guy who was used to people shooting at him. Ava was the whole package, and he couldn't bring himself to keep away.

"When's your flight to Cairo?" he asked, his voice husky.

"Next Saturday, not that it's any of your business."

He studied her, noticing that she still hadn't moved away from him. She enjoyed the game as much as he did. The push and pull. The electricity that always seemed to arc between them. It had been like that since the moment they met, although they'd been flirting, not fighting. "Be careful when you're in Egypt. You know in my line of work we keep tabs on everything—all over the world," he stressed. "It's not the same as the large cities in Europe, where pickpockets are your primary concern. It's dangerous."

"I'll be fine," she said dryly.

"Will you?" he questioned.

"It's just for the summer, Sam. It's not like I'm moving to Cario for the rest of my life. You won't even have time to miss me. I'm sure there are plenty of women to occupy your time while I'm gone for two months."

"Maybe I don't want other women," he growled.

Her face fell slightly for the first time, her voice faltering. "It doesn't matter. I've moved on, and you should, too."

Sam let her turn and walk away, regret churning through him once more. There were plenty of other women he could pursue. She wasn't wrong. But Ava was the one that haunted his dreams. If he was the type of man who believed in settling down and starting a family, he'd want it to be with someone like her. And in reality? Their nights could be so good together. Their days filled with adventures and laughs. Their weekends less lonely.

She might not need a man to warm her bed, but hell if he didn't want to be that guy. Sam didn't have time to smooth things over before she left next weekend, but when she returned?

He wasn't letting Ava get away without a fight.

***

"Ow," Ava muttered at midnight, pausing on the stairwell as her shoes pinched her feet.

"Keep going, sister. Let's have one last toast before we send everyone on their way," Wren said. The women waved one last time to several friends who were descending down the stairwell before taking the rest of the stairs up to their friend's apartment.

"It was so nice of Blair to host tonight," Ava said as they walked in the front door. "I kind of feel like I should have hosted the party since it was my showing."

"No way," Wren said. "We're celebrating you. The guest of honor doesn't need to throw their own celebration. Besides, you know Blair. She was thrilled to plan a big bash and invite everyone she knows. I swear she should've gone into event planning rather than graphic design. And I saw her checking out some of Luke's friends," she added conspiratorially. "Maybe we can all triple date when you're back."

"Ha ha. No," Ava said, rolling her eyes.

"Sam was watching you all night," Wren pressed.

SAM

"Yep. I mean, I won't deny there's chemistry there, but I don't trust him."

Wren frowned, and Ava felt the tiniest twinge of guilt. She knew her bestie wanted Sam and her to get along, but he'd burned her. It'd be embarrassing to repeat the same mistake. No, make that mortifying. "It's like the old saying," Ava explained. "Fool me once, shame on you. Fool me twice, shame on me."

"I don't think he was trying to fool you," Wren hedged. "It was a bad decision. They have stressful jobs requiring their complete attention, and by the time he got back, weeks had passed. He didn't think he should reply."

Ava shrugged, trying to pretend it didn't hurt. "He showed his true colors. Let's have that last toast and head out."

"There you girls are!" Blair exclaimed, her wavy, chestnut hair swishing around her shoulders as she moved toward them. The red dress she had on set off her porcelain skin, and Ava knew more than a few men at the gallery had noticed her this evening. "This was some after-party, wasn't it girls? The drinks and apps at the gallery were fun, but I felt like I had to be on my best behavior with all the wealthy patrons there buying your pieces."

Ava shook her head. "Agreed that some are a little stuffy, but they keep me in business. Some galleries are a little more hoity-toity than others, but it's kind of fun to have my pieces shown in a variety of places. And this? My first solo show? I'm still on cloud nine."

"It was amazing," Wren gushed. "How many paintings did you sell?"

"I sold six tonight, which is really more than I could hope for. They were all large pieces. The gallery director hinted that a few people may come back to look again."

"That's fantastic," Blair said. "I hope you get lots of media attention from this. I know I'll be blasting pictures from the gallery and tagging you in all of them. Maybe The New York Times should do an article on you."

Ava shrugged. "You never know what stories will get picked up."

"If only you knew a reporter," Blair teased.

"Hey, I'll put in a good word for you," Wren promised. "I might be an investigative journalist, but I've got connections. I feel like social media is really what gets the most buzz these days though. Once something goes viral, that's it. You'll get more attention and publicity than you ever dreamed of."

"Absolutely. For better or worse," Ava said, looking pointedly at Wren. Wren's sister had gotten into trouble from posting too much online. Ironically, Wren had tracked her down because her kidnapper had also shared too much. If that wasn't karma, she wasn't sure what was. He preyed on teenage girls but got what was due to him.

Luke and Nick moved past them, helping to grab some empty cups and plates from around Blair's apartment. "Thanks boys!" Blair called out, winking at Nick.

Ava raised her eyebrows.

"Oh, he's a total flirt. Hunky, too. He's kind of got that lethal thing down pat. I wouldn't want to be a bad guy meeting him in a dark alley, but I'd definitely let him pat me down."

Ava snorted.

"He's a former sniper," Wren said.

SAM

"Oh really?" Blair asked in surprise.

"They're all former military," Wren explained. "They served together in the Army."

"And now they work for Shadow Security," Blair mused. "Maybe I should hire one of them as my bodyguard. Nick can thoroughly examine this body before he guards it," she joked, running her hands down the front of her dress.

The women burst into laughter, trying not to laugh harder as the guys looked over. "I hope you're talking about me," Nick called out, waggling his eyebrows.

"You know it," Blair said, blowing him a kiss.

"Sheesh, get a room already," Ava joked. "It was nice of Nick to come tonight. Luke was no surprise since he and Wren are currently inseparable, and as for Sam, he seems to appear wherever I am."

"I'd do him," Blair said, causing Ava to choke on her sip of champagne. "Oh please. I'm just kidding. He clearly only has eyes for you, Ava."

"You're as bad as Wren trying to get us together," Ava said.

Blair lifted a shoulder. "We all remember the stories about the guy you met in Paris. Then you randomly see him in Mexico a year later? It's fate."

"It's bad luck," Ava countered. "And this night is supposed to be about celebrating, so let's discuss something else."

"To a successful, incredible, and amazing night!" Blair said right on cue, raising her glass in the air.

"Exactly. I'll drink to that," Ava said. The women clinked glasses, finishing the rest of their champagne. Ava's gaze flicked around the room. She was surprised to see Sam tying off a trash bag. He and Luke hauled two out the door to dump them down the garbage shoot as Nick grabbed the last of the dishes, stacking them on the kitchen counter.

Fifteen minutes later, they were saying their last goodbyes. Several other friends had just left, and Wren and Luke called out goodnight and hustled down the stairs as well, leaving Ava alone with Sam. How convenient.

She hugged Blair goodbye, thanking her again, and didn't miss the kissy-kissy faces her friend was making behind Sam's back. Ava rolled her eyes, grabbing her purse before walking down the hall in her heels, heading to the stairwell.

"No need to wait for me, princess," he joked, following behind her.

"My thoughts exactly," she muttered under her breath. She slowed down anyway though, reluctantly admitting to herself that walking with Sam was safer than walking alone down the stairs at this hour of the night.

"What's wrong?" Sam asked a minute later, flashing her a look as she gingerly paused on the bottom flight of stairs.

"These shoes are what's wrong," Ava said. "They're like a form of torture."

His gaze landed on her stiletto-clad feet before meeting her eyes once more. Sam moved toward her before she knew what was happening and easily lifted her into his arms. Ava shrieked and clung to him in surprise, looking down the remaining steps. "What are you doing?" she asked.

He leveled her with a look. "Carrying you downstairs. What does it look like?"

"Sam. Put me down," she protested as he easily walked downstairs with Ava securely held in his arms.

"Not a chance, princess. You've been cringing in pain the entire way down. I'm not going to stand here and watch while you suffer."

"You weren't standing there. You were walking down the stairs just like me."

"Touche," he joked.

"I can walk," she said.

"Of course, you can," he replied calmly. "But this way will be faster and less painful for you." He glanced down at her shoes briefly, his eyes darkening. "I dig the sexy stilettos though."

Her jaw dropped, and then Sam pushed open the doors and carried her out onto the sidewalk, looking pleased with himself. "This is all Wren and Luke's fault for rushing out of here," she said.

"They were pretty obvious about it, weren't they?" he mused, gently setting her down on her feet. Ava's hands landed on Sam's forearms, and she found herself staring up into his green eyes as she got her balance. His clean, musky scent surrounded her, and she blinked, finally letting go of him, the moment over. "I'm in a garage down the street," he said. "Parking in Manhattan sucks, but luckily, I found a spot. They'll probably charge me a small fortune, but it was worth it to see your show."

"Sam," she said, hating the way he was looking at her right now. It made her feel all sorts of things she didn't want—not with him, not anymore. She'd dove right into the flames burning between them, and boy, had she gotten burned.

"I'll give you a ride to your place," he said, nodding at a couple walking past them. It was truly the city that never slept, because despite the late hour, there were still cars driving by, restaurants and bars open, and people on the streets.

"I'll catch a cab," she said, taking a step away from him.

"It's the middle of the night," Sam said, frowning. "It's safer if I drive you. I can drop you off before I head home."

"How do you think I usually get around?" Ava asked, growing flustered. "I don't have you chauffeuring me every night. I live alone here in the city, and I'll be on my own all summer anyway in Egypt."

"Promise me you'll be careful in Cairo," he suddenly said, his voice gruff. An unreadable expression crossed his face—concern, perhaps, tinged with something else. Maybe he did care about her in some ways. Sam was a protector, the type of man who rushed headfirst into danger. That didn't mean she was anything special to him though.

"I'll be fine, Sam. Your chance to worry about me was a year ago. I texted as I backpacked around Europe, and you blew me off. Now you don't get any say in the matter."

He shoved his hands into his pockets, staring at her. His green eyes filled with something akin to affection. Fondness. Even when she was arguing with him, he seemed to enjoy it. His gaze licked over her once more, taking in her clingy dress and strappy sandals. She felt the heat of his look like a caress. Ava crossed her arms, trying to shield herself, to hold all her feelings inside.

"You don't get to decide who I can and can't worry about, princess," Sam said, his voice husky.

"I wouldn't waste your time worrying about me," Ava said.

SAM

"I would," Sam replied, his gaze scorching.

Ava bit her lip, her chest filling with an emotion she couldn't explain. He'd drop her off like he'd said—not expect anything, just see that she got safely inside her building. She also knew he wouldn't turn her down if she invited him up to her place.

Ava raised her hand as a cab drove by, and it pulled over a few feet ahead of them. "It might've just been one night," Ava said, looking at him pleadingly, "but you broke my heart. I let you kiss me and touch me—make love to me. You didn't even have the decency to reply to a damn text. It's better if you just forget about me, because I learned long ago that I was better off without you."

A shocked look crossed his face before Sam schooled his expression. Ava turned and walked away, her hips swaying in her tight dress, her hair swishing behind her as she held her head high. She felt Sam's eyes on her as she pulled open the door to the cab, but she got in without a backward glance, like she hadn't just dropped a bombshell that made her own chest ache.

Chapter 10

Sam moved quietly through the crowded bar two weeks later, letting out a deep breath. He used to be all about happy hour with his buddies, but lately, he'd been feeling out of sorts. Antsy. He rolled his shoulders, the muscles slightly stiff. He'd tossed and turned the night before and needed a good night's sleep to feel like himself again. Maybe a good workout first thing in the morning. That was all.

The team had gone on a quick mission earlier in the week, flying down to South Florida to intercept several drug traffickers off the coast. It wasn't their normal type of operation, but the government had wanted answers, believing the men had terrorist ties. A little detour further offshore had landed them the intel the government needed and checked off another job well done for the team.

Sam's gaze swept the crowd. Tables were packed, loud conversations and laughter filled the air, and he

SAM

could make out the crack of pool balls from the tables in the back. A giggling woman bumped into him, almost spilling her beer, and he sidestepped her, frowning.

"Sam!" Ford called out, lifting a hand to get his attention from a table in the corner.

Sam's eyes tracked over his friends. Fucking great. They were there with their women. Luke and Wren sat side-by-side, looking cozy. Ford was with Clara, his arm around her shoulders. Nick had a pretty blonde with him, and Gray was nowhere to be seen. Jett was home with his fiancée and baby. That left Sam as the odd man out.

The blonde woman excused herself as Sam yanked back a chair, heading to the restroom. She waggled her fingers at Nick as she walked away, sashaying off in a tight miniskirt and cowboy boots.

"I thought you preferred brunettes," Luke said, elbowing Nick as soon as the woman was out of earshot. "It sure seemed that way a couple of weeks ago."

Wren raised her eyebrows. "Are you talking about Blair?"

"I wouldn't be opposed to getting her digits, now that you mention it," Nick said. "I just met this girl earlier. You guys weren't here yet, so we had a drink together. I invited her to join us when the rest of the group showed up."

"And now she's plastered to your lap?" Sam asked bluntly.

"Maybe she likes it there," Nick joked. "I don't mind her checking out the goods."

The waitress brought over another round of beers, and Sam plucked a bottle from the tray, taking a long pull. The hoppy brew seeped down his throat as he swallowed.

"Can you bring us one more beer?" Nick asked the waitress, shooting Sam a look. Yeah, he'd taken his buddy's drink but didn't give a shit. His friends had talked him into coming for a beer tonight, so he'd do exactly that—enjoy a goddamn beer.

"You could take your date's beer," Luke pointed out.

"Nah. She'll be back. I'll wait for the waitress to bring another one."

"We can't stay long tonight," Ford said, casually caressing Clara's shoulder with his hand. "The wedding is in two weeks, and we've got to write more thank-you cards tonight."

"Before the wedding?" Sam asked, raising his eyebrows.

Ford shrugged. "People order gifts online nowadays. As soon as we open the gift, we send a note. Otherwise, random relatives are calling or emailing to ask if we received it yet. Clara's got us on top of it all. She's organized like that."

"Shit, I have to get you a gift?" Nick joked. He smiled and thanked the waitress, grabbing the single bottle she'd brought over on a tray.

"Of course you don't," Clara said. "We're just happy that you'll be able to attend the ceremony."

"He's just being an ass," Luke said. "Don't mind him. And I can't believe your wedding is coming up that quickly. Feels like you two kids were just getting engaged."

"Don't I know it," Ford said, smiling at Clara. "A year flew by quickly. I always figured the boss would get married first."

SAM

Clara tried to cover her laughter. "I can't see them rushing to pull off a wedding. Anna is anything but laid back. Don't get me wrong, I love her like a sister, but I have the feeling their wedding will be over-the-top and more than a year in the making. She'll probably want some fancy place in Manhattan that books three years in advance."

"Well hell," Luke said. "They'll probably have a house full of mini-Jetts and Annas by then."

"Goodness, they might," Clara said. "She's excited about her new pregnancy. Jett's worried, obviously, in his typical growly, over-protective manner."

"Yeah, that sounds about right," Sam muttered.

"Anna's calming him down. Their little guy is fussy, but she's as calm as can be. I've tried to give them all the baby tips, at least what I could remember. They'll have their hands full, that's for sure."

"So after the wedding, are you two next? Should I just stock up on boxes of diapers to give as gifts for everything from now on?" Nick joked.

Clara smiled at Ford. "We'll see," she said lightly.

Ford squeezed her shoulder. "We're in no rush. If it happens, it happens. If not, then we'll be a family of three with Eloise. She has been asking for a baby sister though," he said with a chuckle. "At any rate, we'll be official now—legally wed and all that."

"I'm happy for you, buddy," Sam said, eyeing his friend. "And you too, Clara."

"Thank you," she answered.

His friends began chatting more about the wedding and their plans for the summer, and Sam's mind drifted as he thought about his lack of any plan. He'd do the usual—hit the gym to lift, hang out with his buddies, head off on ops. Roll into the office every single morning. He didn't date. He wasn't chasing after women at bars, looking for a good time like he had when he was younger. He hadn't even really taken a vacation in years. He traveled for work, and that had been enough.

Then there'd been Paris.

He took a swig of his beer.

The hurt look on Ava's face before she'd left had slayed him. It was like she'd been pleading with him not to hurt her again, and he felt like the biggest asshole on Earth. If they'd flipped the script, and she hadn't replied to him after the most amazing twenty-four hours, he'd have been gutted, too.

Didn't mean he could change the past.

He took another pull of his beer, realizing that Wren was watching him. She was observant. Sharp. They'd realized that down in Mexico when she'd tracked her sister there from some online sleuthing. She was good at reading people, a trait that obviously served her well as an investigative journalist.

"I heard from Ava," she said nonchalantly. "She's got an apartment in Cairo for the summer. She's already painting," she added, pulling out her phone to show him a picture of the piece. Sam watched as she swiped through a few photos. They were good. He could paint a wall a solid color, and that was about it. She was beyond talented.

"I thought she was doing sculptures," Nick said.

"She will be. There was a delay in whatever materials they were waiting on, but she's exploring Cairo and painting on her own for now. Plus, she's working on the design. Some of the sculptures are for a building in downtown Cairo, so she took photos and measurements to plan what to do in the space."

SAM

"It sounds like she'll be there longer than the summer," Sam said with a frown.

Wren shrugged. "Maybe. I think she'll have some assistants—local art students or something. I'm not entirely sure. Something happened with her cell phone, so she sent me her new number last week. I'll text it to you," she told Sam.

He raised his eyebrows. "Not sure she wants to hear from me while she's gone."

"I think she's homesick," Wren admitted. "Ava was so excited but hasn't even worked on the pieces they commissioned her for yet. It's been a couple of weeks, she has the design, and they're stalling, claiming it's a delay with the materials."

Sam's phone buzzed in his pocket, and he pulled it out, staring at Ava's new phone number.

Wren nodded. "You should text her."

Sam eyed her suspiciously and slid his phone back into his pocket. Of course, Wren was urging him to reach out. She wanted them on speaking terms when Ava eventually got back to the States. Ava would move on at some point if he didn't pursue her. Find another guy. How would he feel if another man was with her?

Pissed off.

No one else should be touching her, making her laugh, seeing that fire in her eyes. And at night? Fuck. It made him see red to even think about another man undressing her, taking her to bed, and hearing Ava's sweet cries.

He'd been an idiot last year. Now Ava was in Cario all alone and just...waiting. Not creating any of the pieces she'd been flown there to work on.

A hint of doubt wound through him as he thought

over the missing phone and sculptures that weren't happening yet. Something about the situation felt off, but he didn't know enough about the specifics to say why. Certainly, ordering materials was understandable. Seeing the space and coming up with a design had probably been built into the timeline.

Sam's jaw ticked as he thought it over.

"Did you miss me?" the blonde asked Nick as she walked back to their table, sliding onto his lap once again. He grinned, snaking his arm around her waist.

"Of course, baby girl. Here's a beer for you," he said, handing her the full bottle.

Sam sat there, listening as his friends started up their conversation again. His phone felt like it was burning a hole in his pocket. Should he text Ava? Make sure she really was okay? He didn't know why Wren was pushing this out of the blue, but if Ava was unhappy there, it wouldn't hurt to check on her. Ava could always ignore him, just like he'd done a year ago, and wouldn't that just serve him right.

***

Sam: Princess, Wren gave me your new cell number. Hope you're staying safe. How's Cairo? The sculptures? I didn't listen to what you said, because I haven't forgotten about you yet.

***

Sam: Princess, it's okay, I figured you wouldn't respond. Wren assures me this number works. Are you making progress on your art? You are so damn talented. I was thinking about you last night. Guess I'm stubborn like that.

***

Sam: Princess, I went to a wedding this weekend. Don't worry, it wasn't mine. ;) The last woman I was with I left in Paris a year ago. I still regret it—letting you get away. That night together was everything.

Chapter 11

Ava squinted up at the bright sun before looking ahead once again, moving along the crowded street. She dodged a man on his cell phone, oblivious to the people around him, and walked behind a couple, taking in her surroundings. Everything was different in Cairo. The food. The clothes. The people. The sounds and scents and even the feel of the air. She'd always loved traveling, seeing the world, and meeting new people, but this was the first time she'd stayed in one place for so long. A new place, at any rate. She'd lived in New York for years, but it was home. Her summer in Egypt was the first time she felt like she was surrounded by a city full of people but without an actual friend.

She let out a breath she hadn't even realized she'd been holding and headed toward the market, planning to do a little shopping that afternoon. While she'd spent the morning painting in her apartment, her creativity felt stifled.

Her summer was different than she'd expected.

The apartment that had been secured for her was fine—small but furnished. It was in a safe area, close to the building where her large sculptures would be installed. Sculptures she hadn't actually gotten started on yet.

Everything was fine. Good, really.

If she felt a little bit lonely most days, that hardly mattered, because she was here to work.

Ava glanced over her shoulder, observing the people behind her. Not for the first time, she wondered if the broad-shouldered man with a short-cropped beard was following her. She'd noticed him when she left her apartment building earlier, lingering around the store across the street. His gaze had locked on hers, but he hadn't moved, just nonchalantly observed her. Ava stood out with her strawberry-blonde hair and fair skin. He wasn't the first person she'd seen watching her.

As for his appearing behind her just now, they probably had been going in the same direction, heading to the center of the city. It's not like she was alone in a dark alley with the guy. They were surrounded by people.

The doorman had nodded at her as she'd left, casually glancing at his watch as if to note the time. It seemed like he'd also been observing her the past few weeks. Casually asking where she'd been, or if she was in for the night. It was his job to watch the building, however. His presence was to make sure everyone was safe, and no doubt he'd been told to look out for her by the wealthy man who'd commissioned her sculptures.

Still. She couldn't deny that the extra attention was a bit unnerving.

Her new phone buzzed in her crossbody bag, and she pulled it out, her heartbeat speeding up as she glanced at the screen.

Sam.

He'd texted her a couple of times over the past few weeks. She'd never responded but somehow felt safer knowing he was there. He wasn't "right there," obviously. Sam was back in New York on the other side of the world. But she was clearly on his mind, what with the semi-regular texts he'd started to send, and Ava didn't know quite what to make of that.

Knowing that Sam cared enough to check up on Ava was something she didn't want to examine too closely. She understood better now why he hadn't responded a year ago after they'd parted ways. Things between them had been passionate and intense—the type of heat and flames some people never found in their lifetime. It had shocked her, too, but in a thrilling sort of adrenaline-fueled manner. She'd always been headstrong and impulsive. Why not dive into a good thing that had come along? They would've been good together back in New York. Maybe they'd have grown apart eventually, but the getting to know one another phase where they ripped each other's clothes off and made passionate love all night would've been oh-so-fun.

But now, on the other side of globe? It was easier to forget about Sam when she was the one in a new, exotic place, away from familiar surroundings. She was living her dream, traveling for her art. She didn't have time to worry about a man.

Besides, it was simply in his nature to be

SAM

protective, and Ava didn't fool herself into thinking she was anything special to him. They had great chemistry. They'd had a night of amazing sex. He wasn't her boyfriend or even a friend. She didn't call him to talk or make plans to see him.

Unable to wait any longer, she swiped the screen to see what he'd texted today. It was nice to hear from someone familiar. She wasn't excited because the text was from Sam.

Not at all.

Sam: Went on a long run this morning. We're heading out on a job soon, so if you don't hear from me for a while, that's why. No need to respond, princess. Just know I'm thinking about you.

Ava paused on the sidewalk, the crowd continuing to move around her. He didn't normally mention when he'd be gone. Was it a longer mission? A more dangerous one? She couldn't fathom why he'd otherwise bring it up. Biting her lip, she decided to shoot him a quick note back. She couldn't ignore him forever. If she wanted him to stop texting, she could easily block his number.

She hadn't.

Thumbing a message back, she quickly hit send before she could change her mind.

Ava: Be safe.

Her phone buzzed right away.

Sam: Always. Be careful in Cairo.

Ava: You know something I don't?

Sam: You stand out anywhere you go. I mean that as a compliment, but it could also make you a target.

Ava: Great. I feel so safe now. :eyeroll:

Sam: I love when you roll your eyes at me, princess. I'm serious about this. Be careful who you trust over there.

Ava: I'm always careful. Even got a new phone number, didn't I?

Sam: What happened with your old phone?

She frowned. Why had she even brought that up? He'd been texting her at this new number for several weeks and hadn't seemed to think much of it. He probably assumed she'd lost it.

Sam: You still there?

Ava: I'm here. Were you always this impatient?

Sam: I've been patiently texting you for weeks, princess. I'm shocked you replied. Now tell me about the phone.

Ava: I still have it. I felt like I was being watched, so I got a new phone. It's not a big deal.

The phone in her hand began to ring, and she cursed. Of course, Sam would worry and call her. She was just being extra cautious.

"Hey."

"What do you mean you were being watched?" Sam asked.

The deep sound of his voice in her ear did something funny to her insides yet also soothed her, and she realized she'd missed talking with him. "Well hello to you, too, sunshine," she said smoothly.

"Ava. Tell me what's going on," Sam said.

She let out a breath. "Hang on, I'm in the middle of the sidewalk here and people are bumping into me because I stopped walking," she said, moving through the crowd. She could see the market up ahead but sat on an empty bench, watching the pedestrians moving past her. The broad-shouldered guy from earlier continued on his way, and she frowned, wondering if he'd stopped when she had. Ava and Sam had been

SAM

texting back and forth for several minutes.

Her eyes followed him, but he turned a corner, disappearing from sight.

"Where are you?" Sam asked.

"A market in Cairo. It's crowded, and I was standing in the middle of the sidewalk texting you. I'm fine, Sam. You don't need to worry about me."

"So what's the new phone for?" he pressed.

Ava brushed her hair back, watching a mother push her child past in a stroller. Another woman rushed over, giving her a hug and beaming at the child. Once again, Ava realized how lonely she was here, surrounded by strangers.

"I'm probably just being paranoid," she hedged.

"Humor me. I do this for a living, sweetheart. It's literally my job to gather info on any given situation. Why don't you explain what happened, and I can decide for myself if you're being paranoid or not."

"I still think you're overacting, but anyhow. I've been here nearly a month, and it started to feel like the people who commissioned my work were keeping tabs on me—watching where I was going, that sort of thing. One afternoon that first week, I set my things down for a meeting. When I came back into the room a few minutes later, I saw a woman holding my phone. She said she'd mistaken it for hers, which seemed odd. We don't even have the same color case. People seemed to be paying even closer attention to me after that, so I decided to get another phone as a precaution. I still have my old one. I just use the new number for texting friends back home."

"Your gut instinct is usually right, princess. If you thought you were being watched or tracked via your phone, you probably were. They could've added tracking software to it and intended to give it back before you noticed. Do you still carry it with you?"

"Well, yeah, because I don't want them to get suspicious," Ava admitted. Her gaze flicked back to the corner, but the broad-shouldered guy hadn't reappeared.

"Has anyone harassed you? Bothered you?"

"No, everyone's been more than polite. Too polite, maybe."

Sam let out a sound, almost like a low growl. "I don't like any of this. Is your apartment safe? The building" Sam asked.

"Of course. The building has a doorman, and I lock up carefully each night. But again, it's not so much strangers on the street that I'm worried about. I've noticed it seems like the doorman is monitoring when I come and go."

"Fuck," he muttered quietly. "Have you started on the sculptures?"

"No. There have been some delays. I've drawn up sketches and taken measurements and photos of the space, but I'm waiting on the materials. It's not a big deal. I'm just chilling in Cairo for a bit until everything is ready. I've bought paints and have been keeping busy that way. I'll get the large sculptures done in the next month or so, add in the smaller ones if I have time, and then be on my way home."

"Do you think anyone's been inside your apartment?" he pressed.

"No, and I don't know why they would. I don't have anything valuable there.

"You. You're valuable, Ava. You're a beautiful, vulnerable woman alone in a foreign country. Do you still have your passport?" Ava sat there, stunned,

SAM

turning his words over in her head. Most men wouldn't care this much about a one-night-stand, would they? Sure, she and Sam had mutual friends, but this felt like more. "Ava," he said when she didn't immediately respond. "They didn't take your passport, did they?"

"No, of course not. I keep it on me at all times in my purse."

"Send me the name of the people who commissioned your artwork," he said.

"What? Why would I do that?" Ava asked.

"I want to look into them. Somethings not sitting right with me," Sam said. "There's no good reason they'd be monitoring you that closely or delaying the start of your project. If the materials were really in that short of supply, they could've postponed it and had you fly over in a month or two."

"I'm free to come and go as I please," Ava said, but she couldn't deny the way her pulse was pounding, adrenaline spiking through her system. Sam was concerned, and that put her even more on-edge. She looked up at the bright sun again, suddenly feeling nauseous. What had she gotten herself into? Ava was a seasoned traveler. She'd been commissioned to do other pieces, although never in Egypt. She looked around at the crowd, feeling slightly lightheaded.

"If you didn't have a reason to be worried, tell me why you needed a new phone." A beat passed, with Sam's words sinking in. "Uh-huh. You were concerned enough to make sure you had a way to contact home without their knowledge. That's smart, Ava. You had good instincts down in Mexico, and I trust you'll be aware of your surroundings in Egypt as well. Follow them. If something feels wrong, that's because it probably is."

"You're kind of freaking me out, Sam," she admitted.

"I don't want to scare you," he said, his deep voice soothing her frayed nerves. "I want you to be cautious. Careful. Are you okay to stay there in Cairo?"

"What do you mean?"

"Hell, princess, I'll come get you if I need to. They might be unhappy you don't complete the sculptures, but screw them. All that matters is your safety."

Ava blinked in surprise. "But your mission. You just texted that you'll be gone—"

"I know what I said. I'll tell Jett I can't do it if you feel unsafe and need to get out of there. We'll fly home together. Hell, we can stop over in Paris if you want."

Irritation began to rise within her. Would he always bring up that day—that night? "That's what this is about, isn't it?" she asked. "You're sorry I haven't jumped back into bed with you and keep hoping that I'll change my mind."

"What? No. I'm worried about you," he said, growing frustrated. "I know how much you loved it there. You said that I was freaking you out, so I was trying to lighten the mood."

"Sam—"

"Trust your gut. If you feel like you're in danger, call me," he continued. "I'll send you Jett's number, too. Wren could always get in touch with him as well. He'll be able to reach me even if you can't."

"I have to go, Sam," she said, her gaze drifting toward the market. "I'll let you know if I'm ever really in trouble, but I don't think you should keep texting me."

"Ava—"

She ended the call before he could reply, shoving her phone back into her bag. Maybe she'd been a bit harsh with him, but damn. She had an amazing opportunity this summer and wouldn't let Sam talk her out of it. Her phone buzzed as she moved toward the market, and she assumed it was Sam sending her Jett's contact info. It would be good to have but not necessary. She didn't need Sam or anyone else to rush in and save her. She'd work on the sculptures and then fly back home at the end of summer as planned. Everything was absolutely fine.

Chapter 12

Sam drummed his fingers on the armrest of the C-17 as they flew across the Atlantic Ocean that night. The team often flew via commercial or private jets, but Jett had arranged for them to hop the military transport to Germany. The next leg of the trip would be on their own. They'd touch down in Damascus and covertly make contact with a U.S. government source, a Syrian national they were helping to exfiltrate out of the country. In exchange for the information the Syrian, Yousef Al Noury, had provided over the years, the man would be relocated to America. Although State would fly him out of the country and escort him onto U.S. soil, the team had to hand him over to U.S. officials first.

The entire region was currently filled with instability and unrest. Although El Din had been taken out of the equation, his successor had risen to power quicker than anyone anticipated. Sam's gut

SAM

churned as he recalled the latest intelligence. The Syrian branch of ISIS was still looking to move weapons to Cairo. They didn't know the names of all the men on the receiving end, which meant they would need to be stopped before the transfer occurred. While they were in-country, Sam and his teammates would gather additional intelligence. If they had enough details to stop the movement of weapons, they'd end this.

It didn't—

"What's up, man?" Luke asked, interrupting Sam's thoughts as he grabbed a seat beside him. Luke tipped back a bottle of water, taking a long pull.

"Eh, just trying to rest up before we land," Sam said. "I can't sleep. Got too much on my mind."

Luke raised his eyebrows. "I noticed. Most of the other guys are out."

"You're not," Sam needlessly pointed out.

"I was thinking about Wren. She was a little more nervous than usual when we left. It's still all new for her—us deploying on missions and being out of contact. Plus, one of her best friends is gone for the summer. You know how the women love to talk."

"I talked to Ava the other day," Sam admitted.

Luke let out a low whistle. "No kidding. How'd that go? I thought she was still giving you the cold shoulder."

"Yep. She was. Ava hadn't responded to any of my texts. I told her I might be out of touch for a while and she actually texted me back."

"Wren's worried about her," Luke admitted. "I got the impression that the summer wasn't anything like she expected."

"It's not. She hasn't even started on the sculptures

yet, and the people who hired Ava are keeping pretty close tabs on her," Sam said with a frown. "I told Ava to send me a name so I can look into the guy, but she hasn't yet. She got annoyed and hung up on me after we talked a couple of minutes. When we get back, I'll reach out again. There's little I can do when we're incommunicado, but I want to research the people she's working for."

"You're worried," Luke said.

"Yep. Didn't Wren wonder why Ava got a new phone number?" Sam asked, eyeing his buddy.

Luke frowned. "No. I was under the impression the old phone wasn't working or something. That's not the case?"

Sam shook his head, briefly explaining what Ava had told him. "If she feels like she's being watched, she probably is. Add in the fact that Cairo is a potential hotspot for terror activity, and it's all I can do not to convince her to come home. I'm worried she's in danger."

"She's a beautiful woman," Luke said. "No disrespect," he added, holding up both hands. "You and I both know that we deal with a lot of sex-trafficking cases. Any chance it's something like that?"

"I don't think that's it," Sam said, shaking his head. "She didn't mention anyone being inappropriate or feeling uncomfortable in that sense. It's more like they're interested in her routine, noting when she's coming and going. It's not sitting right with me. Why are they so interested in when she's leaving her apartment? If she was working on the sculptures as planned, they'd know exactly where she was."

Luke looked thoughtful. "Maybe they're storing

something in her apartment and accessing it while she's gone?"

Sam frowned. "I don't think so. I got the impression that it's sparsely furnished. Where would they hide anything? I suppose there could be a false wall or safe hidden in the floor, but again, why chance that she would discover it? It's not practical."

"I'm just tossing out ideas, man. They could be monitoring her—installing surveillance cameras."

"I thought about that, but she's an artist, not a government official or former military. It's not like she's spilling State secrets or carrying around Top Secret information. I suppose they could have hidden cameras for other nefarious purposes—voyeurism or whatnot. Why fly an American in for that though? There are plenty of beautiful local women if that's the angle. I wish she'd have given me a name, but there's not much I can do at the moment with this whole Mohammad Al Noury shit to deal with. He took over that branch of ISIS faster than anyone could've expected after we took out El Din."

"You saw the new intelligence," Luke said. "They're still trying to move weapons into Egypt. ISIS will increase their stronghold in the region by combining forces with another cell. They'll try to take as many American lives as they can if they're able to smuggle weapons into the country."

"We'll get the data on Al Noury," Sam said with a frown. "His routine, his family, contacts—everything."

Ford quietly walked over, grabbing an empty seat near them. "I couldn't sleep either," he said in a low voice. "Too keyed up to rest."

"You left your new bride," Luke said

sympathetically.

"Yep. I've left her before, but it feels different somehow now that we're official." He shook his head, rubbing a hand over his eyes. "Nothing like being tired but unable to wind down. What do you think of this source we're exfiltrating? It seems odd that the intelligence community wouldn't directly be involved."

Sam lifted a shoulder. "Jett's doing it as a favor to a contact. It's unconventional, but so is he. It sounds like the Syrians were growing suspicious of the intelligence community officers on the ground. They should've been able to get him out unnoticed."

"They were made?" Ford questioned.

"Apparently they weren't very good at what they do," Luke said. "They were probably in-country too long and not as clandestine as they thought. No matter. We'll move in and handle it. After we get Yousef, we'll hand him over to State and then see what additional intelligence we can gather while we're on the ground."

Sam swiped the screen on his phone, looking at the photograph of the man they were bringing in. The new head of ISIS in Syria, Mohammad Al Noury, had a wild look in his eyes and violent aura about him. His brother Yousef seemed calm and almost innocuous in comparison. He wore glasses and was slim, making him appear somewhat weak. Looks could be deceiving, but he didn't have the crazed look of those in the terrorist cell. Sam was amazed he'd been able to pass on intelligence to U.S. officials over the years. He didn't look particularly brave or bold.

"What else do we know about this guy?" Ford asked.

SAM

"He's a scientist," Luke said. "His ties to ISIS are strictly because of his brother's involvement in the extremist group. He's generally flown under the radar, living a quiet life. From what I understand, his brother didn't want to include him—some sort of sibling rivalry shit. Jihad is more important than education, I guess, at least to those assholes. He's the brains of the family and didn't become radicalized like his brother. Most of his career was doing research at a university. His wife and child were killed in an automobile accident earlier this year—mysterious circumstances, from what I understand."

"I wonder if they offed them," Ford said. "If he and his brother have this extreme sibling rivalry or hatred of one another, we can't rule it out."

"It's a good question," Luke said. "There's no telling how deep this contention between them runs. Clearly, Yousef was willing to out his brother and others in the terror cell. He's certainly shown no loyalty to him. Who's to say Mohammad wouldn't target Yousef's family?" He shook his head. "We could get some sleep. We'll be landing in Germany in five hours, and then we'll hop on the private jet. We'll go over mission specifics then and make final plans to locate and bring in Yousef."

"Something feels off about this entire mission," Sam said, uneasiness churning in his gut. "We're sure this guy's been thoroughly vetted?"

Luke eyed him. "He's been an Agency source for years, providing credible intelligence. He's been vetted by both them and State. You sure you're not just worried about Ava?"

"I'm worried about her, but this is different," Sam said. "It feels like something is coming, and we just don't see it yet."

Chapter 13

Ava strode into her apartment after a long day wandering around Cairo, weariness washing over her. She'd picked up some pieces in the market—beautiful handwoven baskets and scarves, a flowy dress, and some smaller items. She was tired, and the doorman's note of her return hadn't made her feel less on-edge. The opposite in fact. He'd been polite but clearly had been watching for her.

Trying to shake off the uneasiness she felt, Ava set her purchases down on the kitchen table. She'd have to buy another suitcase at this rate to get everything home. Aside from the amazing finds from the markets, she'd have all the paintings she'd been working on. The drop cloth she'd been using was folded neatly in the corner, a splattering of sienna, rich yellows, and golden tones upon it. Cairo had some breathtaking sunsets, and she'd taken to painting the city skyline in the evenings.

Her eyes landed on the paintings leaning against the wall. Maybe she would ship them back to the States rather than risk them getting lost or damaged in a suitcase. She rifled through the bags of things she'd gotten today, noticing the woven placemats on her table. Although she wasn't having guests to dine, she'd purchased and set out four placemats, enjoying the splash of color they brought to the room. One at the opposite end of the table was slightly askew, and she frowned, positive it hadn't been that way earlier.

"I must be imagining things," she muttered to herself, setting her purse down. She pulled both her phones out, noticing she'd missed a text from Wren earlier. It had been crowded and loud in the market, so she hadn't heard the phone buzz.

Wren: I miss you, bestie! We're going to have the biggest celebration when you get home. Wine. Apps. The works. Pinky swear!

Ava laughed, remembering how she'd texted Wren that phrase months ago. She'd love to call her up right now to chat or better yet, sit in a quiet restaurant together enjoying a meal and good bottle of wine. Damn. She really hadn't gotten out much here. Dinners alone drew attention, and although she'd had a meal once with her client and his wife, she was mostly eating by herself in her apartment. It was nothing like back home in New York where she'd see old friends, other artists, and Wren and Blair.

Sam's missed text was there as well, but he'd simply passed on Jett's info.

Ava blew out a sigh.

Straightening the wayward placemat, she headed into her kitchen. Ava needed to figure out what to cook for dinner. She should be absolutely famished

SAM

after walking around for hours but surprisingly found herself not that hungry. That's what stress would do to you, she supposed. She grabbed a bottle of water from the fridge and twisted off the cap, taking a long gulp. Ava half-wondered if she was coming down with something. She'd felt a little lightheaded earlier in the day and had been tired in the hot sun. She felt worse after walking inside her apartment.

That's all just needed—to get sick while she was alone in a foreign country.

Ava had expected to be working each day, chatting with the art students, and making new friends. Being left alone in her apartment or exploring the city by herself wasn't the same. Her old cell phone began to buzz on the table, and she picked it up, frowning.

"Hello?"

"Hi Ava, this is Mohammad. How are you doing this evening?"

"Good," she said, glancing at the clock on the wall. It was nearly seven, and it didn't seem like a coincidence that he'd called the moment she got back. Had the doorman let him know she was here? And if so, why? She'd had both phones on her all day.

"My wife and I would like for you to come to lunch with us tomorrow. The materials we've been waiting on for the sculptures will be ready shortly. We'll discuss the final details and make plans to begin."

"Wow, that's fantastic," she said. "I'm ready to begin whenever you are. Will the local students be there to assist?"

There was a pause. "We've had a slight change in plans. Rather than the large-scale installations we've discussed, we'll be requiring smaller sculptures. You'll be able to complete them on your own. I'd like for you to bring them back to New York personally. You'll still get paid the same amount as stipulated in the contract."

"Oh, okay," she said, frowning.

"They will be perfect. I'm certain of it. I'd like to go over the details with you on everything tomorrow. You'll have free reign on the overall design, but there are several stipulations I have."

"I'm not sure I understand."

"The sculptures will all need to be hollow—that will make them easier to transport," he quickly added.

"And the materials?"

"We'll discuss it all tomorrow. That won't be a problem?"

"No, of course not. I was just expecting to be working on large pieces. What's going to happen with the space in the buildings now?"

"I am not certain, but it's no matter now. I'd like to get some of the small sculptures you'll be making to the States. I may have mentioned I have a friend there who is very interested in them. We'll talk tomorrow and discuss it further, Ava. Goodnight."

Mohammad ended the call before she could say anything else, and disappointment washed over her. Getting paid to make the smaller sculptures was a way to earn a living, but she'd been so excited about having her larger pieces displayed in a prominent building in Cairo. If someone in the States wanted them, why on Earth would she fly them in from Egypt? They could've hired her right in New York, saving everyone a heck of a lot of time and trouble.

SAM

Letting out a sigh, she turned back to the fridge. Maybe she'd just skip dinner and call it a night. Hopefully things would look up in the morning.

Chapter 14

Fifteen hours later, the team was on the ground, convened in an abandoned building on the outskirts of Damascus. Their mark was a mile away, and they needed to quietly move in and exfiltrate him in the dead of night, escorting him to the rendezvous point. State Department officials were already standing by, and Sam glanced down at his watch. Their drop was supposed to occur in one hour, barring any unforeseen circumstances. They needed to move in, secure their source, and get him the hell out of Damascus.

Luke spread the satellite imagery and maps on the table as the rest of the men gathered around, looking at the aerial photos. Sam noted the location of the house Yousef lived in and surrounding areas, observing the sections that were densely populated. They'd reviewed everything on the flight but were discussing the last-minute details. It was nearly go-time.

Nick leaned closer, tapping his fingers on the table in anticipation as he eyed a possible sniper's roost. Luke eyed him and then glanced at the others. "Let's go over the final details. The boss said Yousef is being guarded. It's not official, as he can come and go as he pleases, but Mohammad has some of his men living near Yousef's home, watching him. They've been monitoring his movements ever since his brother rose to power."

"They suspect something," Ford said.

"Possibly. We're not sure what would have tipped them off, however, as Yousef's routine hasn't changed. The Syrian's suspicions regarding local U.S. intelligence officials didn't involve him and were related to another incident. Yousef has been living and working in Syria his entire life. The death of his wife and child was months ago. He'd already resumed his job and former activities. There's been no change in pattern that should have raised any concern. With his brother's rise to power in this branch of ISIS, however, it's possible they wanted to keep closer tabs on Yousef and bring him into the fray."

"They're looking for weak spots," Ford assessed. "His vulnerabilities. They want to radicalize him."

"Until recently, his brother's done his damnedest to exclude Yousef," Gray pointed out. "The change is interesting. I wonder if they're planning something and need his help."

"They'll be damn surprised when he's gone," Sam muttered.

"He wants nothing to do with them," Luke said. "He's been a source to the United States for years and is ready to start a new life in America. He's risked his own life by sharing intelligence with us." His gaze shifted toward Nick. "What do you think?"

"I can set up there," Nick said, tapping a finger on the satellite photo. "I'll have a good view of the surrounding area and eyes on the house. The men watching him are there," he said, pointing to a nearby home. "I'll be able to see everyone from that vantage point and can take them out if needed."

"Good," Luke said. "Sam and Ford will keep watch outside, patrolling the area. Nick will be in the sniper's roost. Gray and I will enter the home. We'll need to move quickly, but Yousef understands and is ready to go. He's to have one small backpack with him, nothing more. We're not to disturb anything inside the home. It needs to look like he's simply vanished, not packed up and fled."

Gray crossed his arms over his Kevlar vest, silent.

"You good?" Luke asked, eyeing him.

"Yep—just thinking over the different angles."

Sam eyed his buddy. Gray was more cautious than any of them, having been kidnapped, held hostage, and tortured on their op that went bad during their time in the Army. He didn't trust easily and likely wouldn't trust the man who would be temporarily in their care either.

"We'll drop him with State and move on," Sam said.

Gray nodded.

Luke looked around at the team. "Everyone clear on our entry point? We'll move up the street here as discussed," he said, his finger trailing a line on the image. "If we're spotted, we split up. Gray and I will move toward the house no matter what. Yousef needs

SAM

to come with us tonight at all costs. His life could be in danger, but he has valuable intelligence to share with U.S. officials. We need him alive and well on a flight back to the States."

"Understood," Gray said.

"We'll get him out of there," Ford confirmed as the other men agreed.

Luke rolled up the map, taking one last look at the aerial photograph. He rolled that as well, stuffing both into his rucksack. "Everyone understands the timeline and plan. Let's gear up and roll out."

***

Sam clicked his mic, speaking in a low voice over the headsets as they approached Yousef's neighborhood fifteen minutes later. "Two tangos on the perimeter. They're moving west, away from Yousef's home, but they seem to be doing a check of the immediate area."

"Not sure why they'd be up at this hour. They're not the damn welcoming committee," Nick quipped. He huffed out a breath and then spoke again, a thump sounding. "I scaled the building and am on the roof. I pulled up the rope in case anyone wakes up and sees it. There are multiple homes nearby."

"Roger that," Luke said. "We're hunkered down two blocks away. Sam and Ford will sweep the area before we move in. Over."

Sam jumped down from the wall he'd been standing on and signaled to Ford, and they fanned out on opposite sides of the street, approaching the men from different angles. Luke and Gray remained behind, ready to move toward Yousef's house after the tangos were subdued. If something went wrong, Sam and Ford would provide a distraction so the others could move in and extract their mark.

"I've got eyes on the shorter one," Ford said. "Stocky guy, dressed completely in black. He's searching in some bushes. Not sure what they're looking for, but I don't think we were made. For guys supposedly watching Yousef, I'm not sure what they're doing up at this hour prowling around the neighborhood."

"The street is quiet," Sam murmured. He pulled out his binoculars as he crouched down behind a trash can, pausing to watch the man from a distance.

"It looks like he has a bag of cash," Ford said over the headsets.

Sam shook his head in disbelief. "Strange ass place to hide money. Is he putting it there or taking it?"

"Looks like he was shoving money into the bag to leave it there."

"What's their location compared to Yousef's house?" Luke asked.

"One block over. I don't see the second tango." Sam said, scanning the area. He shifted slightly, looking down the quiet block. "Nick, do you have eyes on him?" he asked.

Static cracked over the headsets, and then they heard Nick's voice. "Roger. He's moving away from Yousef's house, two blocks over, searching under some trees. He's armed."

"We can eliminate them both," Sam said in a low voice.

"I've got the taller man in my sights," Nick told them. "I can take him out if needed. Over."

Sam gestured to Ford again, pointing to the guy

leaving the bag of cash. "Moving in," Sam said. The two men crouched down and jogged along opposite sides of the street, both decked out in full combat gear and night-vision goggles, weapons at the ready.

"Gray and I are behind you, moving toward Yousef's house," Luke updated the team.

The guy in the bushes stood up, noticing them for the first time, and Ford took a shot. The man fell to the ground as they jogged closer. "I got him," Ford said. Sam moved the other way, to where Nick had spotted the taller guard. He jogged down the block, and as the second tango appeared, Sam took aim and shot him in the chest.

"Both tangos down," Sam said, clicking his mic.

"There's got to be thousands of dollars in cash here," Ford said, and Sam heard him searching through the bag.

"Leave it. We need to get Yousef and move," Luke replied.

Gray moved toward the door as Sam jogged back. He watched as Gray knocked once, and Yousef opened the front door. The man looked jittery and slightly panicked. Ford remained outside, standing guard with his rifle as the others moved into the house.

Sam followed his teammates in, rifle aimed ahead of him in case it was an ambush.

Gray was already in the kitchen, searching the bottom level of the home. "Clear!" he called out, rushing down the hall.

"You ready to roll?" Luke asked, eyeing the scrawny-looking man holding his backpack. Yousef's hands were shaking, and he kept looking from the front door to the back of the house where Gray had disappeared. "What's wrong?"

"I want to get my notes. They're in the office closet. It's a blue notebook that I forgot to pack. I just need that, and I'll be ready."

Luke gestured for Sam to grab them, and he hustled down the hallway. Gray was already finishing clearing the last of the rooms. "We eliminated two men outside," Luke said as Sam moved further away from them. He heard Yousef's reply but he was already heading into the office. There were no windows in the room, so Sam flipped on the light switch. He lifted his night-vision goggles to see in the now bright room, noticing how his eyes immediately teared up.

"What the fuck?" Ford muttered.

He blinked and moved to the closet, yanking the door open with a gloved hand. There were boxes of books and papers stacked on the closet floor, taking up most of the space. He scanned the closet's contents and spotted the blue notebook on top of a box. Sam snapped a photo of everything, then grabbed the notebook and moved out of the room, turning off the lights and rubbing his eyes.

Yousef was watching him as he came back into the main living area. Luke was searching through the backpack with a flashlight, making sure they were good to go. All they needed was for their source to turn on them. It seemed unlikely given his help over the years, but you could never be too cautious. Sam handed the notebook to Luke, rubbing his eyes once more.

"Ah. So sorry," Yousef said. "I was cleaning some equipment last week and spilled some of the chemicals. I'd been working on an experiment for the

SAM

university and brought it home. Did you know our food supply would be more nutritious if we added—" He continued to ramble on as Sam exchanged a glance with Luke. Damn academics. He didn't need to hear a thesis on this shit. They needed to move. Sam blinked and them lowered his night-vision goggles, not caring about the food supply chain or the papers Yousef had written about it.

"The house is clear," Gray said in a low voice, moving back toward them. "I didn't disturb anything. It will look like Yousef simply vanished. Even his damn toothbrush is still at the bathroom sink."

Luke nodded and clicked on his mic. "Nick, we're ready to roll out. How's everything look outside?"

"You're a go," Nick said.

"All quiet out here," Ford confirmed over the headsets. "I dragged the bodies out of the way, but they'll be found in the morning. We need to move before anyone gets suspicious."

Luke's gaze swiveled to Yousef, who was now clutching the backpack in his hands. "You're going to lock the front door as we leave and then stay by my side no matter what," Luke ordered. "We'll get you to the rendezvous point and hand you off to State. They'll take it from there and get you the papers you need. If we meet again, it will be back in the States."

"Understood. Thank you," Yousef said. He still looked nervous, but Sam couldn't fault the guy. He was leaving everything he knew behind—his home, friends, neighbors. His work in academia. He'd be resettled in the United States and could start over as a scientist there, maybe get a job at a U.S. university. He'd been starting from scratch in many ways—giving everything up for a new life. The first step was sneaking off in the dark of night as they moved him to a secret location. No wonder the guy was antsy.

Luke pointed to the door. "Then let's roll."

Chapter 15

Ava tilted her head, looking at the bronze accents and other metals Mohammad had provided for her to work with. It would be suitable for the modern pieces, but she couldn't imagine why there'd been a delay in securing materials as simple as that. She'd mistakenly believed he had special supplies for her to use. Nothing here indicated any reason for a month-long delay.

Their lunch had consisted of him giving her specifications for the work. While she'd been under the impression she had free reign, per their phone call last night, Mohammad had requirements as to the size and materials used. Briefly, she recalled how Sam had asked for his name. It had seemed silly at the time, but there were a large number of men hovering nearby at the moment, seemingly interested as she looked over the metals. It made little sense. She doubted they knew Monet or Michelangelo from Jeff

Koons, the modern sculptor. Why would they care what she made?

Uneasiness had filled her stomach all afternoon. The workspace would be suitable, and she could modify her original vision. She couldn't ignore the disappointment that flooded through her, however, at the change in plans. Ava sneezed into her elbow. It figured that she was catching something now when they finally had work for her to do. She sneezed again, blinking as her eyes watered. Good grief.

"What do you think?" Mohammad asked, sauntering over. A large, broad-shouldered man was at his side. Ava was positive he was the man she'd seen yesterday, but she couldn't imagine why he'd been following her.

"This will work," she said in a clipped tone. "I should have everything needed for smaller pieces. Was another artist selected to create sculptures for the building we'd looked at?" She reached for a tissue, blowing her nose.

"Ah—yes," he said smoothly. "They've decided to go in a different direction. Your work is extremely important, however. You'll be able to make these hollow as I requested?"

Ava looked at him quizzically. "I can if that's what you want. Do they all need to be hollow?"

"Yes, that is my preference." Mohammad's phone buzzed, and he glanced at the screen before looking back at her. "You seem dissatisfied."

"I'm just surprised. My commission was supposed to be for larger sculptures, and that's what I'd been designing since I arrived in your country. These are much less complex—"

"You will be paid," he snapped. Straightening his

tie, he seemed to regain control. "I need to take this call. Finish looking at the materials and provide me with a timeline for when the pieces can be completed. I will be back to check in later."

Ava watched in disbelief as he hurried off, the soles of his designer loafers clicking on the concrete floor. The other man walked after him as she was left standing there all alone. Ava walked around the metals, running her hands over the materials. She could do smaller versions of what she'd originally intended. Some of the more intricate design might need to be scaled back as the detail would be less obvious with the change in dimensions. She could weld the pieces together and make some patterns different than what she'd envisioned.

She moved toward her bag at the side of the large room, pulling out a sketchbook.

"What are you doing?" one of the men asked, stalking toward her.

She warily looked at him. "Just sketching some ideas. I've gotten specific measurements to use, so I want the design to look right." He stared at her until she began to feel uncomfortable. The broad-shouldered guy noticed and hurried over, talking rapidly in Arabic. The first guy gave her another hard look but moved away.

"My apologies," the broad-shouldered man said. "I will see that they leave you alone to work."

He was gone as quickly as he'd appeared, leaving Ava again to wonder what was going on. The group of men standing around seemed less refined than Mohammad, who exuded wealth and power. Both times she'd dined with him and his wife, they'd visited fancy restaurants, ordering expensive food and drinks, indulging in whatever they felt like. These men seemed rougher. Harder. Their interest in anything related to the art world was surprising.

The buzzing of her cell phone was a welcome distraction, and she pulled it from her purse, setting her sketchpad down on the table. She smiled as she saw Wren's name flash across the screen, happiness surging through her. "Wren! How are you? I miss you so much," Ava gushed.

"Not nearly as much as I miss you! I'm good. Lonely," Wren added with a laugh. "Ironic, huh? I was used to living alone in Manhattan for years, but the moment my man's gone, it's like I can't get used to the quiet."

"It's an adjustment, I'm sure," Ava said. "Besides, upstate is nothing like the city. Maybe one of your neighbors could honk their horn repeatedly to make you feel at home and give you the finger or pee on your front steps or something."

"Not a chance," Wren said, chuckling, and Ava could imagine her smiling on the other end of the line.

"So, the guys left? Sam texted me that he'd be out of touch for a while."

"They're gone," Wren confirmed. "Luke couldn't say when they'd be back. Honestly, I'm not sure he knew."

Ava was quiet, and Wren continued. "So he's still texting you?"

"Yeah, uh, we actually talked the other day."

"What? You're kidding! Were you going to mention this little detail to me?"

"It was just for a couple of minutes. He said he'd be gone, so I wouldn't hear from him. I hadn't been

SAM

responding to his texts, but this time I shot him a quick text back. We just talked briefly. He was worried about me," she added in a low voice.

"Does he have a reason to be?" Wren asked pointedly.

Leave it to her bestie to cut right to the chase. "The project's a little different than I expected," Ava said quietly. "It'll be fine, but I'm in the studio area now. I can't talk much."

"Why not?" Wren asked, clearly confused.

Ava cleared her throat. "There's just a lot of people around." Her gaze swept the room. The men were still watching her, but they didn't look any more suspicious than they had earlier.

"Call me later on then. Tomorrow if you have to. You still haven't started on the sculptures, have you?"

"They finally got the materials in," Ava said, moving to grab her sketchpad. "Hopefully I'll start in the next couple of days. Listen, I've got to go. I need to figure out the redesign and start sketching out a few ideas, working with the material. We'll talk soon, okay?"

"We better," Wren stressed.

"I promise we will. Love you," Ava said.

"Love you, too, sweetie, and be careful."

Chapter 16

Sam scrubbed a hand over his jaw, leaning back in his seat on the private plane, his teammates seated around him. After three days on the ground in Damascus, conducting surveillance and following the movements of several known ISIS members, they still didn't have details on when the movement of the weapons would occur. It was concerning. If they'd been able to find a location where the munitions were being held, they could've raided it. Ended things. The planned ISIS operation was being kept tightly under wraps. They'd never gotten eyes on Mohammad Al Noury either. No doubt he was being careful given that his predecessor had been taken out. He was lying low, and rightfully so. The man was smart enough to realize he was a high value target.

"That drop was neat and tidy," Gray said from across the aisle. "We didn't get all the intelligence we hoped for, but handing off Yousef went seamlessly."

SAM

Sam's gaze flicked to his buddy. "You were worried."

Gray nodded. "If he'd been caught, he'd have been tortured and killed. They don't take kindly to traitors."

"Or finding the enemy snooping around—us," Sam added needlessly. He hadn't missed the way Gray had stiffened as he spoke. The guy had demons he never talked about. He held his own on missions, and Sam trusted his buddy with his life, but Gray's scars were both physical and mental. He didn't let anyone get too close and would never trust easily. Sometimes Sam was amazed Jett had convinced him to join Shadow Security at all.

"I was worried about the possibility Yousef would turn on us," Gray admitted. "Something seemed off with the men prowling around at night. What the hell was that bag of cash for?"

"Jett's not too happy about that loose end," Ford agreed, leaning toward them. "Our job was to extract Yousef, but no doubt Al Noury's men retrieved the cash."

"Or some other lucky asshole," Gray said. "There were houses all over the place."

"It's not like the bag would've had someone's name engraved on it," Luke pointed out. "We would've kept the money from whoever it was intended for, but that wouldn't give us anything to go on. Yousef was the priority."

"Let's just hope Yousef has more intel on the rest of his brother's operations," Gray muttered. "Stopping the weapons shipment would've been the icing on the cake for that op."

"What the fuck kind of cakes have you been

eating?" Nick joked, causing the others to chuckle.

Gray smirked but shook his head. "Dick. The military can move in when we have the necessary intelligence, but it would've been nice to end this shit while we were there—wrap everything up in a nice fucking bow."

"It's never ending," Ford muttered. "We knock one guy down, and another springs up, like a sick game of Whack-a-Mole or something."

"You okay?" Sam asked, eyeing his buddy.

"Good. Just missing Clara is all," he added sheepishly. "She worries when we're gone too long. It'll be good to get home."

"She's got you by the balls," Nick said with a smirk. "Who knew sweet Clara could have big, bad Ford eating out of her hand?" He elbowed Ford, trying to egg him on.

"Jesus," Sam said, shaking his head. "You're probably next, dude, with the way everyone else is shacking up these days. Didn't you get Blair's number?"

"That I did, but you're hardly one to talk," Nick said.

Sam lifted a shoulder. "I'm single, buddy."

"Yeah, but the difference is, you don't want to be." Sam mulled that over as his friends continued ribbing one another. Sure, Ava was on his mind. Ever since they ran into each other again, it's like the floodgates had opened. He was always thinking of her, the careful walls he'd built around his memories tumbling down, cracked open by a tiny strawberry-blonde. His mind began to drift, stuck on a memory from Mexico a couple of months ago when they'd fled the burning nightclub.

SAM

Ava looked up at him with fear in her eyes, but Sam gripped her hand tightly. "We have to get out of here, princess."

"But Wren—"

"Luke will take care of her. We need to split up from them in case we're being followed. I'll get you back to the hotel."

She nodded, those big blue eyes wide, and hurried along at his side, pressing close. He shifted his grip on her hand, wrapping one arm around her slender shoulders. Ava was so much damn smaller than him. He could push her to the ground and shield her with his body if needed. Protect her no matter what.

Sam glanced back over his shoulder and then moved her along, his gaze sweeping the area.

Ava clung to him as they crossed the busy street. A small flicker of warmth filled his chest. She might still be angry at him, but deep down, she trusted him to keep her safe. She hadn't protested, hadn't fought him. She'd simply let him get her away from danger.

Sam hailed a cab and held Ava close as it came to a stop.

"You're trembling," he said quietly.

"We could've been killed in that explosion," she whispered urgently, growing upset. Sirens still wailed in the distance, the blaze lighting up the night sky, and as Ava looked up at him, he swiped a stray tear that rolled down her cheek.

"Don't cry," he said gruffly.

"I'm not. I'm fine," she said, taking a deep breath and steeling herself. She swiped at her tears as Sam's big hands gently gripped her shoulders, steadying her. Their eyes locked for a moment, their connection undeniable even then. Ava was so close, her soft curves almost pressing up against him. Her lips parted in surprise as Sam strained to hold himself back.

He'd almost kissed her. He'd almost fucking kissed her right there on the street in Cancun. It was so wrong as far as timing went but also could've been so right. The cab came to a stop and that was it. The moment was over. He'd helped her to climb inside, and then they were on their way, Ava trying to hold herself together.

"Did you ever get a full name for the guy?" Luke asked.

"Huh?" Sam asked. Clearly, he'd missed out on most of the conversation. His teammates had been talking as he'd let his mind wander. Now everyone was looking at him, the plane quiet.

"The man Ava is working for," Luke clarified. "I called Wren when we stopped in Germany, and she'd spoken with Ava a few days ago. I guess Ava mentioned you wanted to look into him."

"Not yet," he said with a frown. "I figured I'd touch base when we got back to the States." Sam scrubbed a hand over his jaw, thinking.

"Mohammad's a common name," Luke said.

"What?" Sam asked, his gaze flashing to his friend.

"Wren thought the man's first name was Mohammad."

"Mohammad?" Sam asked, irritation rising within him. "Shit. What if it's Mohammad Al Noury?"

"The leader of ISIS in Syria? Don't be crazy, man," Gray said. "That name is as common as hell in the Middle East. It's like the name John in America or something. It's not the same guy."

"Ava never gave me a last name," Sam pointed out.

Luke frowned, looking between the two men. "See what you can find out from her when we land. Get a last name. I agree, however. His first name alone means nothing. It's too common to be anything but a coincidence. Besides, she's in Cairo. Yousef told us that his brother was in Syria. They want to move weapons to Egypt, but there's no reason he'd physically go there."

"Yeah. You're right," Sam said, shaking his head. "I still don't trust this guy—whoever her Mohammad is. He hired her to make some fancy sculptures in downtown Cairo and then had her sitting around for weeks with nothing to do."

"Why is that?" Gray asked, looking confused.

"There was a delay in securing the materials," Sam explained. "But Ava thought they were closely watching her."

"She's an attractive woman," Gray said.

"That's not it. She ended up getting a new cell phone because she was worried they'd bugged the old one or were tracking her with it. She's an artist. They'd have no reason to closely monitor her like that."

"Huh. That does sound odd. But she's staying there in Cairo even with nothing to do?"

"I offered to come get her," Sam admitted. "I'm sure she doesn't want to quit the job, but last we spoke, she hadn't even started it yet."

"Are you worried she can't leave Egypt?" Ford asked, looking over at him.

"I honestly don't know what to think. There are a lot of red flags. I'd feel better if she were back in the States, but that's not my call. As Ava none-so-delicately told me, I lost my chance to have any say in what she does."

"You sure have a way with the ladies," Nick said.

Sam muttered a curse and took a swig of his water. He was tired and sore from trekking around Syria and didn't need his friends razzing him. He was worried about Ava though. Something was off about the situation, and he was determined to get to the bottom of it.

Chapter 17

Ava let out a frustrated sigh as Mohammad narrowed his gaze at the sculpture. His jaw ticked, and she could tell he was irritated. She'd spent hours working on a delicate, ornate piece. It met his size specifications, using the metals he'd secured. It was airy and beautiful, not to mention easy to transport back to the States.

"No, no, no," he said, walking around the large work table. "I should have told my men to check on you while I was busy in my meetings. The sculpture should be hollow, yes, but this is all wrong. It is too open. I need an enclosed piece with a hollow interior."

She tried to maintain a neutral expression as he continued talking. The small sculpture was decorative and evoked the feel of previous pieces she'd done. Had this man never seen her work before? Although she was known for her paintings, she enjoyed working in other mediums from time-to-time. Ava had wrongly assumed he was familiar with her work and had liked her prior sculptures. Why else would the man hire her and fly her to Egypt? She was becoming more well-known in the art world, and even if he'd never seen her pieces in a gallery, her online presence was strong.

Not for the first time, she recalled Sam asking her what she knew about this man. She didn't want to admit he might've been on to something. Sam probably thought she was foolish for doing so little research on the man she was working for. The chance to work in Egypt had sounded amazing—the opportunity of a lifetime. Someday, God willing, she'd settle down and get married, have two point five kids and a dog. Live a different life. This was her shot to grow as an artist and dream big. She'd wander the world, traveling wherever life took her before finally settling down.

"Ms. Kincaid?" Mohammad asked, and she realized she'd been daydreaming.

"This is the style I've come to be known for," she explained, trying not to lose her patience. "My sculptures are delicate. Ethereal. They convey movement through their lines and openness. They would've been perfect for the lobby as originally intended—not too imposing but prominent enough to fill the space. A nice balance of artistry and strength."

"I understand, but as I am commissioning these pieces, which will now be housed in New York, I want them to look exactly as I request. After these are done, perhaps we can get back on track with the large sculptures. I will have final say in the design of these.

It will need to be redone according to my exact specifications."

"Of course," she said as she turned away, rolling her eyes. Good lord. Most people would be thrilled to have an artist design a custom painting or sculpture for them. It made no sense to hire someone if your vision didn't mesh with their style. She'd taken the job before her solo show in New York, but Ava had assumed he was familiar with her work.

Clearly, she'd been mistaken.

"Is there a problem?" he asked when she didn't say anything else.

Ava cleared her throat. "Of course not. I can start anew, as long as you don't mind a delay. I was under the impression you'd seen the sketches and were okay to move forward. I'll have the redesign ready for you to look at tomorrow."

"My men did not show the sketches to me," he said, muttering something else under his breath. "I only saw the original plans for the large sculptures."

"My mistake," she said, eyeing him curiously.

The door opened, and two men walked in carrying a large box. A faint chemical scent filled the air, and she sneezed. "Cleaning supplies," Mohammad said by way of explanation, glaring at them. They quickly turned and left, taking the box back out of the room with them. Ava looked back to Mohammad, realizing he was watching her closely. "I expect to see some good progress on this," Mohammad finally said, effectively dismissing her.

He turned and stomped out of the room, lifting his phone to his ear when he was near the door. "What is it?" he barked. "Yes. Yes. There was a delay, but we'll be back on track. We have everything we need." He switched to Arabic and then disappeared through the doors. Ava was left standing there alone with her work and wondering, not for the first time, how she'd gotten herself into this.

***

Sam's hands moved over her gently. Possessively. He cupped her bare breasts, his eyes hazy with arousal. "You're so pretty, princess. Are you wet for me?"

"Always," she murmured, recalling the other ways he'd taken her. Missionary. Doggy style. And now Ava was perched atop him, Sam eyeing her like she was his next meal. His big hands squeezed gently, his thumbs rubbing her nipples. She moaned before gazing down at him, taking in his bulging biceps and broad pectorals. She was ready to rub herself all over him.

"Lift yourself up," Sam said, his hands moving to her hips. "I want you to ride me."

Ava shifted to her knees, and then Sam eased her back down. She gasped as his thick cock notched at her entrance and then filled her, stretching her completely and reaching every hidden place inside. He was big and thick. Throbbing.

"Sam," she breathed, gasping at the feeling of fullness.

"You feel so good, princess," he said, bucking up into her slowly as she gasped in pure pleasure.

She uttered a low cry as his thumb slid to her clit, pressing gently, and then he was claiming her once more, thrusting harder as she surrendered to him.

The buzzing of Ava's phone on her nightstand caused her to jolt awake, gasping in shock. One hand reached over to the empty spot beside her in bed, half expecting to find Sam there. She was humming with arousal, her pussy throbbing. She blinked as her eyes

SAM

regained focus and took in the dimly lit room of her apartment in Cairo. It was dark outside, but she'd left a lamp on, not expecting to fall asleep.

It had been a dream. Just a dream.

Her nipples were hard, her panties damp, and skin flushed. It had felt so damn real, like he was really there with her.

Her phone buzzed again, and she reached over, fumbling with it. As she picked it up, she was shocked to see Sam's name on the screen. It was only ten p.m. her time, but she'd been exhausted, falling asleep almost as soon as she'd gotten home. It'd still be daytime back in the States, and briefly, she wondered why he was calling rather than texting her. Were they back from their mission? Was everything okay?

"Hello?" she asked, her voice husky with sleep.

"Hey, it's me. Sam," his deep voice rumbled. "Did I wake you? Sorry, I figured you'd still be up."

She blinked, still in somewhat of a daze. "Oh. Yeah. It's okay," she mumbled. "I fell asleep earlier but hadn't really gone to bed yet. I left most of the lights on in my apartment. Is everything all right?"

"Yes," he assured her. "Everything's fine. We just got back." He cleared his throat when she didn't say anything. "I just, uh, wanted to follow up. You never sent me the name of the man you're working for."

Ava let out a breath, staring up at the ceiling. It felt intimate to be talking to Sam while she was under the covers, still half asleep. This was clearly a business call though, strictly for information. Sam and his teammates worked for a security firm. He wanted to make sure she was safe because that was his job. She might not have hired him, but he was the type of man who protected others.

And if his voice stirred something inside her?

She certainly wasn't about to tell Sam she'd been having a sex dream about him. Ava wasn't even sure where that had come from. She'd been busy earlier dealing with Mohammad, stressed about redoing the first sculpture. It was like her subconscious couldn't shake Sam even if she wanted.

"Ava, are you still there?" he asked.

"Yeah, sorry. His name is Mohammad Badr. He's a businessman in Egypt and owns a couple of buildings in Cairo. He said he has an affinity for art and the finer things in life."

"Are you positive that's his real name?"

"Well, I didn't demand to see his driver's license or passport if that's what you mean. That was the name on the contract I signed and how he introduced himself. His people sent me plane tickets and got me settled into an apartment here in Cairo, so clearly, he's got money from somewhere."

"I'll do some checking into things, see what I can find out. Have you started working on the sculptures yet?" he asked.

"Yes," she said, blowing out a sigh. "It's actually been kind of a disaster. He wanted me to modify what I've already done. The first was too open and airy or something," she muttered. "This was supposed to be my design, but he has multiple specifications about what he wants. It's bullshit. I'm an artist, not an architect or something. I should be given some latitude in how my pieces look."

Sam quietly listened to her rant. It wasn't the type of thing they usually talked about—not recently, at any rate. They'd spent hours together in Paris while she excitedly told him about the paintings they were

SAM

looking at and pieces she wanted to work on. He'd never complained or looked bored, just seemed happy to be with her.

Ava turned that thought over in her mind. The man had literally spent an entire day following her around Paris as they enjoyed each other's company. Going back to her hotel had been Ava's idea. She jumped in headfirst and gotten burned.

"So, what exactly does he want the sculptures to look like?" Sam asked, confused.

She briefly explained their earlier conversation. "The first day was weird, too," she admitted. "Mohammad showed me the materials, and several men were in there watching everything I was doing. I went to get my sketchpad, and one guy hurried over to question me."

"You're still being watched," he said bluntly, sounding unhappy.

"Sort of. No one was in there today. I was left on my own to work, which is what I prefer, to be honest. I was supposed to have art students helping me, but I'm no longer making the large pieces that would require assistance. Mohammad checked in with me late this afternoon and was upset about the sculpture I'd started. He basically wants me to start from scratch. I thought this would be fun, inspiring work, not dealing with a micro-managing businessman who clearly knows nothing about art."

"Have you felt unsafe at all?" Sam asked gently.

"Just wary, like everyone is watching me. There are always different men hanging around. I'm not sure what they expect. It's not that exciting to watch me work. I'm not painting nude models or something."

Sam chuckled. "I'd watch you work, princess."

"Sam—"

"I know. I don't have the right to call you that. Answer me one question though—do you really never think about me? I screwed up, but that connection we had? Hell. Chemistry like that doesn't happen often. And then to run into each other again a year later in Mexico? Have our best friends move in together? It's like I can't stay away from you even if I wanted to—which I don't. Not anymore."

"I'm on the other side of the world, Sam. Even if I forgave you, which I haven't, that doesn't mean we should be dating. The timing is wrong all over again."

"You won't be in Egypt forever," he protested. "I'm going to convince you to give me another shot."

"That's awfully confident of you." She looked up at the ceiling again, feeling so close and yet so far from him. She didn't hate Sam flirting with her or pursuing her. He was as hot as he'd been a year ago. He listened when he was actually there, and their chemistry was one hundred percent real. But getting hurt again? That part she didn't think she could handle.

"You haven't moved on either, Ava. You don't have a boyfriend. And yes, like I said, I asked about you."

Her heartbeat sped up. "And what did you find out?" she asked softly.

"Just like I'd told my buddies about the woman from Paris, you'd told your friends about me. You were so excited that we'd met until I ghosted you, and for that, I'm so fucking sorry."

"I feel like I can't trust you," she admitted.

"I know, and that's on me. There's no rush, princess. When you're back, we'll go out. No

SAM

pressure. I'll pick you up and drop you off like a perfect gentleman. We'll take it slowly. I'll even let you drag me around to all the art galleries in New York."

"I don't know…."

"Think about it. I needed to get my head out of my ass to see what was right in front of me. I know you don't need me—you're incredible. A talented artist who's independent and could get any guy. I don't want you to be with other men, selfish as that makes me. I want you for myself. By some stroke of luck, you're still single. Hell, maybe you were waiting for me to find you again and didn't even know it. Just give me a shot, sweetheart."

His words washed over her, soothing something inside. As far as she knew, he hadn't been dating anyone either, but could she really take a chance with him? Nothing about it felt simple. "Maybe," she finally replied.

He chuckled, the deep sound winding its way through her insides, warming her entire body. Sam could make her melt like no one else. The way he'd watched her when they made love—he'd been so careful. So thorough. She'd never shied away from sex, but it had been passionate and intense with him. A joining of two people who seemed destined for each other. And when he'd pinned her beneath him, staring deep into her eyes as they made love, he'd forced her complete and utter surrender.

"Maybe? Whew," he joked. "You're making me sweat over here."

"Well, it wouldn't be the first time," she teased, recalling their sweaty bodies tangled together between the sheets.

"Now you're killing me," Sam said, but she could hear the amusement in his voice.

"You really just got back today?" she asked.

"Affirmative. We dropped off our gear, checked in with the boss, and I headed home. Haven't even showered or slept yet. I told you I'd check in on you when I returned."

Heat bloomed within her. Sam's attention was flattering. Comforting. He made her feel safe, even from thousands of miles away. "I remember that you said that, but I didn't think you meant the instant you were back."

"You're important to me, Ava. I know I didn't make you feel that way before, but I swear that it's the truth."

"You kept me safe in Mexico," she admitted.

"And I'll keep you safe in Egypt, too. Just let me look into this guy, and we'll see where we're at. We can move forward from there when we have additional information."

A knock sounded on her front door, and she startled at the interruption, glancing in that direction. "Sam? I gotta go. Someone's at the door."

"This late? Are you expecting anyone?"

She shoved the covers down and stood up, glancing down at her athletic tights and camisole, hoping she didn't look too disheveled. "Well, no, but I'll look through the peephole and see who's there. I won't answer if I don't recognize them. Really, I can't imagine who'd be coming around at this time. They're probably just at the wrong apartment."

"Keep me on the line," he ordered.

"Geez, you're so bossy," she muttered, padding across her bedroom.

SAM

"Always."

"All right, I'm going to the door now. I'll be sure to tell you if it's an ax murderer or something."

"Not funny, princess."

She tried not to roll her eyes. His protectiveness was sweet but also unnecessary. There wasn't much he could do from New York. As she walked through her living room, she realized she felt better than she had earlier. She'd been sneezing and watery-eyed again this afternoon, working in the industrial space. After being home and taking a nap, she felt remarkably improved. Ava quietly went to the door and looked through the peephole, surprised to see the doorman standing there. "It's just my doorman," she said quietly into the phone. "Hang on."

She opened the door a crack, peeking out, phone still in hand. The doorman lifted a paper bag up. "Mohammad asked me to drop this off," he said.

The delicious aroma of Egyptian food filled the air, and her mouth watered. "Thank you," she said, opening the door further and reaching out to take it from him.

"It's heavy," he said, moving through the doorframe. "I'll put it down for you." She stiffened, unsure what to do as he strode inside. It was late to be bringing food. Just because she'd slept through dinner didn't mean anyone else would know that. The doorman set the bag on the table, his eyes tracking over the area. He did a double take as he spotted her other phone lying there. Ava's fingers tightened on the one she was holding, Sam quiet on the other end.

"Two phones?" the doorman asked, raising his eyebrows.

Ava nervously swallowed, pressing back against

the open door. "Everyone has multiple devices—phones, tablets, laptops. It's not a big deal."

He looked down at the phone and then at her again. "Then you won't mind if I give Mohammad your other number," he said in a low, threatening tone. "Why don't you tell me it right now?" She stilled, her lips parting in surprise as he chuckled. "That's what I thought. You're hiding something."

"I'm not hiding anything," she protested, her heart racing.

He raised his eyebrows. "You didn't have two phones when you arrived in Cairo."

"How on Earth would you know that?" Ava asked, multiple scenarios running through her mind. Had this guy been searching her apartment? Gone through her things?

"Mohammad said you didn't look happy to be starting over with his sculptures," the doorman said, his gaze dropping to her chest. Suddenly, the camisole and athletic tights she'd put on earlier made her feel like she was wearing next-to-nothing. Icy cold dread snaked down her spine. He licked his lips, smirking as he stalked toward her. "Do all Americans dress like whores?" he asked.

"What?" she asked in surprise. "You need to leave right now. I didn't invite you inside."

"If you wish for me to keep your second phone a secret, you'll do something for me first." His gaze flicked over her darkly.

"Ava. What's going on?" Sam asked over the phone.

The doorman seemed to realize someone was on the other end of the call. "I'll let you know. And I won't take no for an answer."

SAM

"Ava? Who the fuck was that? Did he just threaten you?" Sam asked angrily over the line. The doorman had already walked out, brushing past her, and Ava was breathing heavily, quickly locking the door behind him. She latched the chain and stepped back, as if getting away from the door would somehow protect her from whatever was coming.

"That was the doorman for the building," she said breathlessly. "He walked inside with a bag of food before I could stop him and saw my other phone on the table."

"What did he say to you?"

She bit her lip, walking over to the food that he'd left and eyeing it suspiciously. "He saw my other phone on the table and suspected something. I don't know how, but he knew I didn't have two phones when I arrived in Egypt. Then he asked me if all American women dress like whores."

"I'm going to kill that motherfucker," Sam said darkly.

"Sam."

"Does he always speak to you like that?"

"Never. I wouldn't have stayed if I felt threatened before. He was always watching me as I came and left the building, but that was the extent of it. What am I supposed to do tomorrow? I can't just work on the sculptures and act like everything is fine. I can come up with an excuse for having two phones, but now they know about it. I don't know what's going on," she said, hating the way her voice trembled. "I'm worried they're involved with something bad, and I'm missing the big picture. I'm not sure how the doorman fits in other than I think Mohammad owns this building."

Sam muttered a curse. "I'll fly to Cairo. Hopefully Mohammad is just some shady counterfeit art dealer or something and it's nothing worse, but I have my doubts. I'd book you a flight out of there myself, but I'm concerned they'd follow you to the airport. They're using you for something, and we need to figure out what. Call in sick tomorrow. I'm going to have the team research Mohammad when I'm on the flight. Do you know the doorman's name?"

"No, but I'll find out."

"Do it. Don't let anyone else in, and don't eat the food they sent you."

"Seriously? Never mind. I have other food. I've eaten dinner with Mohammad and his wife before, so them sending delivery isn't entirely out of left field, but it's still strange."

"Throw it out and stay in your apartment. I'm going to book a flight right now. If there's nothing commercial, Jett can get me on a private plane. Will you be okay tonight?"

"Yeah, I should be. What can you do anyway? You're on the other side of the world."

"We've got contacts everywhere, princess. You have Jett's number. If something goes wrong while I'm in the air, call him. We'll get someone to you. I don't know all the people he does, but I'm coming for you."

She heard Sam moving on the other end of the line, opening and closing drawers. Was he already packing a bag? He'd just gotten home from God knows where and was coming to Cairo to help her. "I'll text you my flight information and ETA as soon as I have it. Stay put until I get there. I don't think I can take anything happening to you," Sam said, his voice filled with emotion. It made her chest clench. Sam was the type of man who fought hard and protected the people he cared about. She'd known he was dangerous back when they met in Paris, and she had a feeling she was about to find out exactly how much.

"Maybe I should start packing so I'm ready to go when you get here."

"Yep. Pack your stuff. Best case is I can get a flight out immediately, but you know the drill. I'll be in the air almost eleven hours. Call in sick in the morning. They won't be able to stop you from leaving when I'm there. Whatever the hell they have you involved with doesn't matter, because I'm getting you out of there."

Ava jolted and looked over as someone knocked on her door again. "Shit. I think he came back. I won't answer the door."

"Tell me who's there. Don't open the door, just look through the peephole."

"Okay. Hang on." She shoved the bag of food aside and started to walk over, crying out in surprise as the door was suddenly opened. The chain caught the door for only a moment, and then it was kicked in with a loud thump. Ava screamed as two armed men stormed inside.

Chapter 18

"Ava! What's happening? Ava!" Sam yelled. The call ended, and Sam immediately called her back, cursing as it went straight to voicemail. He swiped the screen, pulling up her old number, but knowing in his gut that she wouldn't answer that call either. The old number rang and rang as he paced his room. "Shit!" he cursed, tossing his phone onto his bed in frustration. She'd been talking to him one moment, and then there was a loud crashing sound as she screamed. His blood had run cold knowing she was in danger. Sam didn't even know where she was staying in Cairo. He didn't know her address, section of the city, or anything.

Had the doorman come back for her? Mohammad? She'd said he'd been unhappy at her not making the smaller sculptures to his specifications. He grabbed his phone again, adrenaline coursing through his veins as he called Luke. Wren would know where

SAM

her best friend was. After speaking with them, he'd call Jett. Their boss had contacts all over the world. Maybe he could get someone to go look for Ava. Sam needed to get to Cairo ASAP but feared it would be too late.

Luke's phone rang several times before he finally answered. "What's up, man? Miss me already?"

"I think Ava's been kidnapped," Sam said, his voice terse.

"Kidnapped?" Luke asked, suddenly all business. "What happened?"

Sam briefly gave him a rundown, Luke shouting out to Wren before Sam had even finished explaining. "I'm putting you on speaker," Luke barked. There was a rustling in the background and then Wren's panicked voice.

"Sam? This is Wren. What's going on?" Her voice was shaky, and his gut churned at the urgency of the situation.

"Someone broke into Ava's apartment while I was on the phone with her," Sam explained, trying to control his anger. He heard Wren quietly crying as Luke soothed her. "I'm sorry. I know she's your best friend, but she's in grave danger. Do you know where she's staying in Cairo? I've got the name of the man who hired her, but that's it. I don't know anything else."

"Yeah, I've got the address somewhere," Wren said. "Let me look through my texts." Luke said something to her and then was back on the line.

"I'm going to Cairo," Sam said.

"Call the boss. I'm going with you. Jett can get us a private plane, which will be faster than dealing with the airlines. What do we know about this asshole?"

"Absolutely nothing. Ava was vague on the details before she left for Egypt, and I just got his name tonight. Mohammad Badr. She finally started on the sculptures, but Badr was unhappy from what she told me. They've been watching her closely the entire time she's been in Cairo. It's shady as hell. Some asshole threatened her tonight when he discovered her second phone. Shit," he muttered. "I should've told her to get out of there a week ago. I sat on getting intel on him, and now she's fucking gone."

"This isn't your fault," Luke said. "Ava's a grown woman who can make her own choices. You asked for a name before, didn't you? She chose not to tell you or research the guy herself. We'll use the info we have now and move forward with it. Oh, great," he said, talking to Wren. "I got an address for Ava."

"Send it to me. We'll search her place when we get there and try to figure out where they took her. It sounded like they smashed the damn door in, so the police are likely involved as well."

"Unless they're on the payroll for these guys."

Sam swiped a hand over his face, muttering a curse. "Everything's a possibility. At least we have a starting point now. We need to know where she was working. She wasn't making the sculptures in her apartment. We'll get the dirt on Mohammad Badr and hopefully some other addresses. Somehow the doorman is involved as well, but I don't have a name for him yet."

"We'll get her back," Luke assured him. "Pack your stuff and meet me at headquarters. We'll need to bring equipment and weapons."

"Roger that. I'm calling Jett now."

Sam finished stuffing clothes into his duffle bag as

SAM

he moved around the room, eyeing the dirty laundry he'd dumped on the floor. He'd been back mere hours and needed to leave again. His mind was whirling, spinning in a hundred different directions. He scrolled his contact list again, pushing the call button.

"Jett here. What's wrong?" his boss asked.

"Ava was attacked in Cairo. We were on the phone just a few minutes ago, and someone broke into her apartment. Luke and I are going after her."

"Motherfucker," Jett ground out. "Did you know who she's working for?"

For the first time, Sam was glad his buddies had been busting his balls about Ava. Their boss knew exactly who Ava was and that she was in Egypt. Sam didn't have time to start at the beginning and explain the whole damn story. "Mohammad Badr. The name didn't ring any bells, but I'm not up on Egyptian evildoers," he muttered. "Supposedly he's a businessman in Cairo."

"I'll get West on it right away. Badr's bound to be a wealthy man if he flew Ava into Cairo for the summer. While open-source intelligence might show he's on the up-and-up, we'll get to the bottom of it. What do you suspect?"

"Not sure, boss. He has her making sculptures, and he's very particular about how they look. She's not doing the large pieces she was commissioned to work on either. He's requested smaller ones, and the materials he needed were delayed for over a month. He's hiding something, but I've got no idea what the angle is or how Ava fits into it. They broke into her place tonight and took her," he said, growing frustrated.

"I'll call in the team," Jett said, and Sam could hear him moving down the hall. "We'll meet in the conference room ASAP. You and Luke aren't going alone."

"Understood."

"We'll find your girl."

"She's not my—"

"Bullshit. You've been hung up on her for a year, and don't think I didn't notice. We'll find Ava and then have a nice welcome home party at my place when she's back. Pack your bags. I'll see you in thirty."

Jett ended the call before Sam could say another word, and he cursed, looking around his bedroom. Ava could be hurt, scared and alone somewhere in Cairo. They could be raping or assaulting her. Worse. It could be too late by the time he arrived, and he'd never see her smiling face or big blue eyes again. Never pull her close and kiss her like he wanted.

Sam punched his duffle bag, hating the way it gave. He wanted to beat the shit out of something, but he'd have to wait until they were in Egypt. He'd never forgive the assholes over there if they'd hurt Ava. He'd find her no matter what, and after that, he'd end them.

***

Sam paced back and forth in the conference room as Jett barked out orders over the phone. While the team had the day off, having just returned from their mission, Jett had already been at headquarters.

"Roger that. They'll be there. Be ready to take off at seventeen hundred." Jett ended the call and looked

SAM

over as the rest of the team hustled into the room and took seats at the long table. Gray had just showered, his hair still damp. Nick was in workout clothes. Ford and Luke hadn't even changed yet, still wearing the clothing they'd flown back in.

Sam yanked back a chair, nearly knocking it over in his haste. He was keyed-up, adrenaline coursing through his veins. The last thing he wanted to do was sit still. Sam felt ready to jump out of his own skin. He wanted to get to Ava, shoving aside anything and anyone in his way.

"We got a flight out in one hour," Jett said in a clipped tone. "The pilot is on standby while they fuel up the jet. The ground crew is already onsite. Ford and I will remain at headquarters with West and the IT guys, running things from here. The rest of you are on that plane to Cairo."

"Roger that," Gray said, and Nick nodded. Sam and Luke already sat tense and alert in their chairs, ready to rush down to the armory once the team had finished their briefing. Sam felt agitated and restless, knowing the clock was already ticking. They needed intelligence and gear, however, in order to move in and save Ava. As much as he hated it, they needed to prepare, not rush in blind.

"What do you need me to do, boss?" Ford asked.

"Get with West. I may need you to find out some additional information. West's on his way over from a different meeting but said he has something for us to see."

"Already?" Sam asked in surprise.

"It's not about Mohammad Badr," Jett said darkly. "The intel pertains to Yousef. He might have ties to this in a way we didn't expect."

"The guy we just exfilled?" Gray asked in disbelief, clenching his fists. "Motherfucker. I knew something was off about him."

"What's the connection?" Luke asked.

Jett looked down at his phone again. "That's West calling." He swiped the screen, pushing a button. "West, you're on speaker. Tell us what you found."

"I was in a meeting with officials from State. We were going over some technical specifications for another op when this came up in the conversation. There's footage from Yousef's interview with the Feds. His brother was trying to recruit him to join ISIS. They needed his help with a new operation."

"God damn," Gray muttered. "I knew it. Remember the bag of cash? I bet they were bribing him—or attempting to, at any rate."

"To do what?" Ford asked. "And why would they leave it hidden outside?"

"So we wouldn't find it. Maybe he told them we were coming or they somehow found out about it. They needed him for their terror plot but knew he was meeting with us."

Sam shook his head. "That makes no sense. He didn't bring the cash with him or even try to retrieve it. And he's not in Syria anymore. They bribed him to what—leave the country?"

Gray slanted him a look. "Maybe he's plotting something here."

Jett's gaze darted between the two men as he mulled that over, his jaw tight.

"I'm sending you a video," West said, and Sam's eyes landed back on Jett's phone. "I'm not supposed to have a copy yet, but after I heard about it, I, uh, borrowed the footage from the Feds."

Jett muttered a curse. "Go on."

"Stand by. I'm sending it now. It's a large file, so check your encrypted email."

Shaking his head, Jett ended the call and flipped open the laptop at the end of the table. He quickly typed in his password and pulled up the message, casting the screen of the laptop onto the large TV at the front of the room. "Here it is," he said, clenching his jaw. Jett moved the cursor over the stilled video image in the email and pressed play.

Sam sat up straighter as they saw Yousef seated at a table with several officials from State. The footage was somewhat grainy from the surveillance camera in the room, but the sound was crystal clear. "It is urgent that I give you several updates," Yousef said, looking at the men and women across the table from him. "My brother is plotting something against the United States with a terror cell in Egypt."

"Yes, we're aware of the potential terror plot between ISIS in Syria and the Egyptian branch," one of the men in a suit said, watching him closely. "What additional information do you have?"

"My brother has been traveling back and forth, overseeing the new operation. Mohammad tried to involve me, and I refused. For most of my life, he wanted nothing to do with me. There's no reason why I would help him now. I wanted to go into hiding, but as you know, I was being watched by his men. I gave up everything I've ever known to relocate to the U.S."

"You've been a valuable asset over the years," the man replied.

"Where has your brother been traveling?" a woman asked.

"From Syria to Cairo. There are multiple players

involved—not just ISIS. They're working with other men who share a hatred of the Western World and want to harm as many Americans as possible."

Sam stilled, leaning closer.

"Did he smuggle weapons with him during these trips?" one of the men asked.

"He's planning to. I believe he was waiting on certain supplies. My brother didn't give me all the details given my refusal to help. I know some of his plans, however."

"What else can you tell us? How is he planning to smuggle weapons into the States?" the same man asked, crossing his arms.

"He's not smuggling guns or bombs, which would set off metal detectors at the airports and show up in x-rays of luggage. He's working with chemicals—creating chemical weapons."

"God damn," one of the men said. "What type?"

"I'm not entirely sure," Yousef replied, looking nervous. "I refused to help and don't know what his decision was. My brother planned to conceal the chemical weapons and then have his connections here in the States unleash them on the unsuspecting public."

"What's he concealing them in?" the female agent asked, leaning closer.

Yousef cleared his throat. "I believe he hired an artist. He's going to hide them in sculptures and have them placed in buildings throughout New York City."

Chapter 19

Ava whimpered from the corner of the large room, her wrists and ankles bound with rope, her mouth gagged. Her cheeks were stained with tears, her throat raw from screaming earlier. The men who'd broken in to her apartment had subdued her after she'd tried to run. She'd woken up alone, seemingly unhurt, but scared out of her mind. Had they drugged her? Knocked her out? She didn't remember anything after they'd tackled her to the ground, holding her in place as they tied her up. One of the men had covered her mouth as she'd screamed, and then...nothing.

Sneezing, she looked around, realizing this was the same building where she'd worked on the sculptures. She recognized the metal walls and faint chemical scent in the air. She sniffled again, her eyes watering. She was allergic to something in this damn building. Why had they brought her here? And who were the men who'd burst into her apartment?

She pulled at the restraints on her wrists, frustrated. If they were going to hurt her, to rape or kill her, she couldn't sit around and do nothing. She needed to free herself in order to fight them.

And Sam?

Her eyes filled with tears again. He'd been on the phone with her. He'd know something had happened and come looking for her. But would he get here in time? Damn it. She hadn't even given him her address yet. Wren had it. Thank God. This whole thing had been so close to being over. Sam was supposed to fly over and help her safely leave, keeping the men who'd been watching her away.

She shifted, wiping her tears with her bound hands.

Loud voices in the hallway caused her to stiffen. Ava cowered back as the door suddenly opened, Mohammad himself coming into the room. A shadow crossed his face, and he looked irritated to even be here at this late hour. She tried not to let him see her trembling but couldn't stop her body from shuddering as the door closed behind him, leaving them both alone.

"Ms. Kincaid. It seems we meet again." He strode toward her, his eyes flicking over her clothing. She'd had on jeans and loose, flowing tunics the other times they'd met. Her workout clothes were skintight. And she hadn't even worked out, doing her usual yoga in the evening. She'd fallen asleep as soon as she'd changed into the camisole and stretchy pants.

Ava trembled as he moved closer. "I'm going to remove the gag from your mouth," he said, his expensive loafers echoing on the hard floor. "Screaming will do you no good. As you are already aware, this building is soundproof. We wouldn't want to disturb anyone while you complete the sculptures," he added with a chuckle. He knelt down in front of her, and she leaned back, the strong scent of his cologne overpowering. He reached around her head, roughly untying the knot of her gag. It fell from her face, but Mohammad didn't move away. He lifted a section of her strawberry-blonde hair, rubbing a strand between his fingers as she cringed.

"What do you want from me?" she asked, pulling away. She could hardly fight him with her arms and legs bound, but maybe she could stall whatever he had planned.

"I can see why my men are so intrigued by you. You're a beautiful woman, Ms. Kincaid."

"Why did you bring me here?" Ava asked, hating the way her voice shook.

He chuckled as he let go of her hair and stood, pacing in front of her. "You have observed more than you should. That is my fault, perhaps, but an issue we now need to remedy, nonetheless." He reached into his pocket, and she realized he had both of her cell phones in one hand. "What is the meaning of this?" he asked. "Suddenly you have two phones?"

"One's personal, one's for business."

He threw them both to the ground, and she cringed as the screens shattered. "My men tracked your contacts. You have connections to many members of the U.S. military. Why is that?" he asked, his gaze narrowing. "Are you working for them?"

"Of course not. I'm an artist."

"My men confiscated your phones and looked into your last incoming calls. The man you were last speaking with is former Army, as are several other of the contacts you have saved. It seems like no mere coincidence."

"That doesn't mean anything," she protested. "Lots of people serve in the military."

"I'm not sure I believe you," he said, smirking. "Either way, you've seen too many of my men and too much of what is going on. You will finish the sculptures you've started for me. We've had enough delays as it is, and I need them completed. After you finish them? Well, my men can fight over you if they want, but you won't ever see your country again."

"No!" she said stubbornly.

He raised his eyebrows. "I have all the control here. You were brought in tonight because you witnessed something you shouldn't have."

"The box they had earlier," she murmured. "The chemicals." Shock washed over her. What were these men really doing in this industrial space? And how the hell did it involve the sculptures she was making?

"Ah, now you're remembering more. I'm a prominent businessman in this country, but I work with all types of people. I can't have you asking questions, especially given your connections back in the States. You will remain here and finish the job."

"No. I won't do it."

"No?" he asked, amused. He was a predator toying with his prey, and she hated feeling weak and helpless, bound before him.

"People will be looking for me. I signed a contract to work here for the summer. The embassy knows that I'm here. You won't get away with this."

He smiled, moving close to her again. "It was a shame, the invasion at your apartment earlier. What are the chances? A single, American woman alone in a foreign country. You had no chance against the armed intruders that broke in. I was kind enough to send you dinner, and late that same night someone came and attacked you. People will ask questions, but it's already been taken care of. You were targeted and robbed. Killed." He glared at her. "No one will be looking for you. You will work on the sculptures for me tonight and stop wasting my time."

She stared at him, stubbornly refusing to answer.

"Would you prefer I turn you over to my men now?"

Mohammad barked out an order in Arabic, and several men came into the room. "Who shall I hand you over to first?" he asked.

"I'll help you," she quickly said, and he flashed her a knowing look. "That's what I thought. I will have my men untie you, but they're not to touch you without my authorization. If you refuse to cooperate? Well, that is your choice. You'll have to deal with the consequences for your disobedience." He began talking rapidly in Arabic again, and she wished she could understand what he was saying. He wasn't a businessman interested in art. It was a cover for something. Drugs? Weapons? The chemical smell was odd, but they could've been cleaning up, covering their tracks. What was he hiding?

Mohammad finished talking, and one of the men walked over, roughly yanking her to her feet as she gasped. Ava fell against him, still bound, and he pulled out a knife, cutting the ropes free from her wrists. Ava rubbed her raw skin as the man knelt down, his hand gripping her calve tightly as he cut the rope from her ankles.

"Get to work," Mohammad ordered. "I need these

sculptures done and shipped off. You were to have brought them back to the States yourself, but you're off the hook now. It will make my job harder but is one less thing for you to do. You will remain here, working for me in Cairo, Ms. Kincaid. You are never leaving Egypt."

Chapter 20

"This is the latest SITREP," Luke said, slapping a map and report on the small table of the private jet as the team flew over the Atlantic. Sam shoved the laptop he was using aside, moving over to his teammates.

"Jett had West do a deep dive into Mohammad Badr and his men. Badr is a prominent businessman in Cairo but has well-hidden ties to ISIS. His primary motivations are money and power. Badr was paid royally by the terror cell to help smuggle weapons into the U.S.—chemical weapons. Although his plans originally involved an American artist—Ava—making sculptures to conceal the materials and bringing them into the country herself, he will have to find someone else to carry them in now."

"That's messed up," Nick muttered.

"I still can't believe Ava got herself involved in any of this," Sam said. "I should've insisted she let me research the guy."

"The past is in the past," Luke said. "Let's move forward with where we are now. She's in danger, and we have the opportunity to stop Badr's plan."

"What about the shipment of weapons from Syria to Cairo?" Gray asked. "Were the weapons we were looking for all along chemical weapons?"

"Intelligence analysts assess that yes, that is the case," Luke said. "Mohammad Al Noury was able to smuggle the chemical weapons during his travels back and forth between Syria and Egypt. They're now in the hands of Mohammad Badr."

Sam shook his head. "These two Mohammads are confusing as hell."

"Mohammad Al Noury is head of ISIS in Syria. Mohammad Badr is an Egyptian businessman. Two different men, both intent on harming Americans," Luke said.

"Got it. Al Noury moved weapons from Syria to Cairo. He wanted his brother Yousef involved because he's a scientist."

"That's the assumption we're working under, although Yousef didn't have specifics given his refusal to help," Luke told the team. "We don't know how they procured the chemical weapons, but Al Noury was able to hand them off in Cairo. A terror cell there recruited Badr. With his wealth and connections, he was able to hide in plain sight, hiring Ava and moving forward with the plan."

"Except they grew to suspect Ava," Sam said. "She was wary about the situation, and they were watching her closely enough to figure that out. Jesus," he murmured, rubbing a hand over his eyes.

"We'll find her," Gray said, his voice lethal.

"There's not a chance we're leaving Egypt without Ava on the plane with us."

"I just hope it's not too late," Sam replied.

"We'll have to search her apartment when we land," Luke continued. "It's in this section of Cairo," he said, pointing to the map. "No doubt Badr's men will have it watched. Ava believed the building was owned by him, which will make entering unnoticed tricky."

"But not impossible," Nick said with a smirk.

"We'll get in," Gray confirmed.

"While Nick and Gray search her apartment, Sam and I will be investigating Badr's businesses. West got us a list of properties owned by him in Cairo. We need to figure out which is the most likely location for them to have brought Ava. They'll want her to finish the job," Luke said. "It'll be a warehouse or industrial type of building, not an apartment. If Badr needs her to complete the sculptures, that's most likely where she's being held."

"God damn it!" Sam swore, frustrated.

Luke leveled him with a look. "You need to calm down and keep your head on straight. Ava needs us. We'll pore over the businesses now and make a list of the places we want to investigate. We can conduct surveillance when we're on the ground. Once we narrow it down, we'll move in."

Sam was breathing heavily but nodded, hustling back over to the laptop he'd been using. He tapped at the screen, typing in his password again. "I see West's email. Hell, this guy owns a lot. Let's divide up the possibilities. We can look at sat imagery to determine which might be a good spot for housing this operation and hiding chemical weapons."

"Let's do it," Luke said.

***

Ava watched as the man helping her attempted to weld the pieces of the sculpture together. It was a nightmare, ruining the delicate details of the piece and leaving a big glob of molten metal at the edge. He cursed and ranted in Arabic. If Mohammad wanted these to look artistic, it was a complete failure. The man helping her had botched the job, making it look like a child had made it, not a talented artist.

"No, no, no!" Badr said as he stormed in. He yanked the man helping Ava out of the way. "No one would believe I paid an artist for this," he seethed. "These all need to inconspicuously pass through airport security. This will never make it on a plane because it will be thoroughly examined."

The man apologized, bowing slightly.

"You will have to do this yourself," Mohammad snapped at Ava. "I will have one of my men watching you the entire time. You are dismissed," he told the man backing away.

Ava glanced nervously across the room. They'd been up for hours, and her eyes stung, both from the chemical residue in the air and lack of sleep. All of the metals Mohammad had procured were stacked in a corner as well as boxes of whatever he planned to use.

"Isn't it dangerous having that here?" she asked.

He chuckled. "It's reactive. Nothing will happen until another easily made ingredient is added. When the time is right, my men will see that these are in working order." Ava eyed him warily. The carefully constructed persona he'd always had around her seemed to be crumbling. There was nothing but evil and greed in his eyes now. "I can see you doubt me," he said with a smirk. "I was paid a lot of money to get these into place, and the idiots I have working for me won't prevent that from happening. You are proving to be a valuable asset, Ms. Kincaid."

He stepped closer, looming over her, then smirked as she stepped back. "I need you for your artistic skills, not your American pussy. My men, on the other hand…." He shrugged carelessly. "If you fail to do as I ask, you will be passed around to them."

Ava tried to school her expression, hiding the shock that coursed through her. Mohammad was nothing like the polite businessman she'd met when she first arrived. He'd been hiding his evil, sinister side. Was his wife in on this, too? Or did she have no idea what was happening? Maybe he was wealthy enough that she just didn't care.

Mohammad called out something in Arabic, and she froze as the doorman from her building walked in.

"I see you recognize Ahmed," Mohammad said. He began speaking in Arabic again as the doorman moved inside, watching her. Ava shivered in her camisole, taking a step back. Mohammad smirked again and then strode out, not bothering to say anything else to her. The threat was clear. She was to do what they wanted, or the doorman would do what he wanted with her.

Chapter 21

Sam hustled off the plane in Cairo, his pulse pounding as he slung his rucksack over his shoulder. The flight had taken too damn long. He'd wanted to rush in immediately, which was impossible with Ava on the other side of the world. Even if he'd been in country, he didn't know where Ava was being held. All he could do was sit tight over the long-haul journey across the Atlantic and review the sat imagery and locations of properties owned by Badr. They made a list of targets, and adrenaline coursed through his veins at the prospect of getting her back. Each step was one closer to Ava, and Sam needed to hold it together and not lose his shit before Jett yanked him off the op entirely. He'd go rogue if he had to but knew he was better off with the entire Shadow Ops Team at his back.

Gray hustled down the steps behind him, hefting a bag of weapons in one muscular arm as they moved

SAM

onto the tarmac. Jett had arranged for the team to land in a private airport, hopefully not drawing too much attention to themselves. Jett's contacts all over the world were valuable, and Sam was grateful as hell to his boss for getting them where they needed to be ASAP.

"Body armor's in here," Nick said, jogging over to where they'd gathered with a large duffle bag. Sam dropped his rucksack down, turning to help his teammates. They all needed to pitch in and make haste. He needed to compartmentalize his feelings—to not think too much about Ava, just focus on the mission. The job.

"Grab the comm's equipment," Luke ordered.

Sam nodded and hustled over to pick up the gear, his thoughts churning. The latest update from Jett had made his blood run cold. The local police had reported a string of burglaries in the apartment building Ava had been living in. Her disappearance was officially linked to those—an unfortunate result of the crime-spree. It was a cover-up, no doubt, but clearly intended to throw the public off course. The embassy was involved given that Ava was an American citizen, and Badr was willing to do anything to throw them off his tracks. He'd been playing the concerned landlord and prominent businessman, promising to help search for the American woman himself and even offering up a reward. While Jett could certainly bring the embassy up to speed, it was better for the team to handle this alone. The element of surprise was a benefit to any mission.

"He's a sick fuck," Sam muttered.

"Badr?" Luke asked. "He's arrogant enough that he won't be expecting us. That works to our advantage."

Gray swiped the screen on his phone, frowning. "The media is camped outside Ava's apartment building. That'll make it more of a challenge for Nick and I to slip in. We're not going in through the front door."

"I'm always up for a challenge," Nick quipped.

"We're going to check into a hotel in downtown Cairo to stage the rescue," Luke told the men as they stood near the plane. "We'll go over the final details and will do some preliminary scouting this afternoon. A rescue will most likely need to occur under the cover of dark, unless we determine Ava is in imminent danger."

Sam growled beside him, hating the idea of Ava being stuck somewhere for even another second. "Of course, she's in danger," he spat out.

"We need to be careful," Gray needlessly told him. "I know she's important to you, but we can't fly in there blind and get her injured or killed."

"Got it," Sam muttered. He knew the drill as much as any of them. It killed him to know the woman he cared about could be hurt, helpless and alone. Nearly fifteen hours had passed. Anything could have happened. Yet it was currently broad fucking daylight in Egypt, and they needed to be inconspicuous when they moved in to rescue her. Waiting until nightfall was like a punch to the gut. The element of surprise was key, however, and he begrudgingly knew his teammates were right.

"Remember our cover," Luke warned them. "We're old college buddies looking to backpack around Egypt—see the pyramids and all that shit."

"Yeah, yeah," Nick muttered. "Let's get this show

SAM

on the road."

"You got someplace better to be?" Gray asked.

"If you must know, I got a text from an old flame yesterday. We sporadically kept in touch over the years, but this was out of the blue. I need to call her."

Sam raised his eyebrows. "That doesn't sound like something you'd do—at all."

Nick lifted a shoulder. "I'm not a total screw-up. This girl and I were dating when I first joined the Army. It didn't work out because we were young and dumb, but she reached out to me this week. She wanted my help. I did shoot her a text back, but she wanted to talk. I'm not one to carry a torch, but hell. If I believed in fate or that shit, she was it."

"Did you hit your head or something?" Sam asked, baffled.

"No, asshole. I'm just trying to do right for an old friend."

"An old girlfriend," Sam corrected.

"You'll have to worry about her later," Luke said in a clipped tone, gesturing for the men to hustle. "That's our ride. We'll set up in the hotel and pinpoint Ava's location this afternoon, gathering all the intel we can. Tonight, we're getting Sam's girl."

***

Ava blinked as she awoke, curled up in the corner of the room where she'd been working. She'd fought sleep for as long as she could, wanting to protect herself, but after nearly pulling an all-nighter, she'd given in to her body's need for rest. She wasn't sure how long she'd slept, but she was still groggy. Exhausted. One sculpture was nearly complete.

Mohammad's men would place chemicals inside, and they'd solder the final piece on, making it smooth and impossible to detect that anything was hidden within. It would be a beautiful sculpture capable of harming others if put in the wrong hands. She didn't understand what he meant about adding an agent, but she knew certain chemicals would react when combined. Would it create some sort of gas? Could it cause an explosion? Ava was an artist, not a scientist, and she was completely in over her head.

Bile rose in the back of her throat. The idea of innocent people being hurt because of her made her sick. She forced herself to sit up, leaning back against the wall, and saw the doorman asleep at the table where she'd been working. So much for guarding her. He was completely out. Her gaze shifted to the table itself. The first sculpture was gone, she realized, and her heart dropped. Were they already preparing to ship it to the States? She was helpless to stop them.

Her eyes tracked around the room, wondering when Mohammad or his other men would return. It was odd that her only guard was now sound asleep. Should she try to sneak out? No doubt the others were around here somewhere. If she got out of this room, then what was next? Would she be able to leave the building?

Ava's focus shifted back to the sleeping man. What if he had a phone on him? Could she send a text to Sam? She'd memorized his number as a precaution the other night. Was he already looking for her? Even if Sam couldn't get here, he'd have notified the American Embassy or one of their contacts in the region. Someone would be trying to find her.

Quietly, she stood, remaining in place for the

SAM

moment. She felt grimy and gross from sleeping on the dusty floor, but that was the least of her concerns. She was a prisoner of some sick terrorist group that was intent on harming Americans.

Ava needed to get out of here.

She licked her lips, her throat dry. They'd given her neither food nor water since kidnapping her from her apartment, not that she'd feel safe taking either from these crazed men.

Ahmed, the doorman, was still sleeping soundly as she looked back over. If she could get his phone, there'd still be the problem of unlocking it. Hopefully he didn't bother with such things, but Ava knew this might be her only chance to contact someone. She had to try. Steeling herself, Ava took a small step forward. Ahmed didn't move, and she began to quietly tiptoe across the room. Hesitating at the table, her eyes ran over him. He wasn't in his usual doorman's uniform, instead wearing pants and a shirt. The idea of reaching into his pocket to grab his phone made her cringe, and she wasn't even certain he had it on him. She placed her hand flat on the table beside his head, and he didn't flinch, still breathing heavily.

Her gaze dropped to his waist, trying to see if she could locate the phone without touching him. She reached out slowly, gingerly patting one of his pockets. Nothing. Ava shifted, walking quietly to his other side. His face was toward her now, still resting on the table, and she felt her pulse pounding. Ava broke out into a cold sweat, terrified as she froze in place. Even if she got the phone, how would she get it back in his pocket?

She didn't have the chance to try.

Ahmed's eyes suddenly flew open. He blinked at her, hesitating for only a moment, before he pounced. Ava shrieked as he snatched her wrist, holding her in place. "What are you doing?" he asked, his voice deep with sleep.

"Nothing. Just wondering what's next. The sculpture is gone." He didn't release her but sat up straighter, looking around. His grip tightened on her wrist as he finally stood.

"You were looking for something."

"No," she protested, trying to pull away.

"You're a big asset to Mohammad's operation, but he's not here," the doorman said darkly, swinging her around and shoving her back onto the table. She shrieked as her back wrenched and head hit the solid wood, stunning her.

"Wait," she pleaded, holding up both hands. Her eyes frantically darted around, looking for anything she could use as a weapon. He took a step closer, still gripping her wrist with one hand but using the other to pull her legs apart.

"He'll be furious that you're doing this," Ava said, suddenly feeling calmer. "He hired me to work for him, not you."

"He's an idiot," the doorman spat out. "He's had me watching you all month. Certainly, no man can resist temptation for so long. I won't tell him that you were sneaking around in here, but you're going to give me what I want."

"No," she whimpered.

He was on her in an instant, his hand covering her mouth, his large body pinning her in place. Ava kicked at him, trying to fight. She bit at his hand as he cursed, and then rough fingers were at her waist, trying to yank down the tight athletic leggings. Ava wrested away and screamed, the sound echoing around the room.

The door suddenly slammed against the wall as it opened, several men rushing inside.

"Get off her!" Mohammad yelled, followed by a string of what sounded like curses in Arabic. "I need her in one piece to finish the sculptures. You can play with her afterward for all I care. In the meantime, she is not to be harmed!"

Ava was crying and shaking, and she pushed past Ahmed as she stumbled off the table.

"Bring her some food!" Mohammad barked, and one of his men disappeared back through the door. Mohammad's dark eyes landed on her. "You will eat and then get started on the next sculpture. We've wasted too much time as it is. Get him out of here!" he yelled, pointing at Ahmed. The other men dragged him out as he apologized to Mohammad, and Ava wrapped both arms around herself, trying to hold it together. Her trip to Egypt had become a complete and utter nightmare, and she prayed someone would get to her before it was too late.

Chapter 22

Sam and several of his teammates stood around the small table in the hotel room, looking at the map of Cairo. After scouting out several buildings earlier and relying on additional information from West, they'd determined the location they believed Ava was being held.

"All of the materials were delivered here," Luke said, pointing to a building across the street from their mark. "Badr owns the building and has offices there, so someone would have been available to receive the shipment even if the warehouse was empty."

"And metals and other materials needed for sculptures aren't exactly subject to scrutiny," Sam muttered.

"Exactly. Everything shipped to him was perfectly legal. The chemical weapons smuggled in from Syria are another story. We'll have to worry about how he acquired those another day."

SAM

"After receiving the shipments, they moved everything from Badr's office building to the warehouse across the street," Gray said, his eyes narrowing at the aerial photograph beside the map. "He's owned the warehouse for five years. What else does he use it for?"

"We believe he's smuggling goods—artwork and jewelry for the most part. Somehow, he was recruited by ISIS. Now he's moving weapons. They'll pay him a significant sum if the sculptures containing chemical weapons are successfully delivered to New York."

"Jesus," Sam muttered. "Ava suspected something was wrong while she was here in Cairo, but hell. You'd need some kind of out-of-the-box thinking, Red Cell analyst group to come up with a terror plot like this. If she had any inkling as to what they were planning, she'd have been on the first flight out of here. I was coming to bring her safely back myself. They moved in too quickly," he said, scrubbing a hand over his face.

"We'll have her soon," Gray said, shooting him a look of understanding. Gray knew more than anyone what Ava was going through. He'd been held hostage—tortured. It was unlikely Ava was receiving similar treatment, but she was a beautiful woman. It was possible she'd been assaulted, and the very thought of harm coming to her felt like someone was twisting a knife in Sam's gut.

"I just got off the phone with Jett," Nick said as he hurried over. "Guess he's at home now. I heard a baby screaming in the background," he added with a shake of his head. "Jett's got the pilot on standby. Once we rescue Ava, assuming she doesn't require medical attention, we're good to fly out."

"We retrieved some of her personal belongings," Gray added, nodding toward the box, backpack, and suitcase at the side of the hotel room "We were able to recover most of her paintings. Ava's a hell of an artist."

Sam nodded, his fist clenching. He just hoped Ava would be alive and well to see them for herself. If anything had happened to her—no. He couldn't go down that line of thought. She had to be okay. Anything less was unacceptable.

"Let's finalize our plans. Two of us will approach from the back of the warehouse," Luke said, pointing to the north side of the building on the photo. "That's going to be the easiest point of entry as far as moving in undetected."

"I'll remain near one of our getaway vehicles down the block," Nick said. "I'll keep eyes on both buildings and update the team via our comms units if anyone tries to exit or enter. I'll take them out if they try to move Ava to a new location."

"I'm counting on the element of surprise," Luke said. "We'll subdue them before they even know that we're there."

Gray shifted, looking down at the photo and map. "I'll breach the building from the west side, near the loading docks. When they moved deliveries from across the street, that was how they brought the materials in. They may try to exit through that side if they realize we're there."

"We don't know what type of chemicals are being stored inside the warehouse," Luke said, clearing his throat. "If we accidentally shoot something containing them, it's possible none of us will survive the explosion. We'll subdue or take out any armed

SAM

men that we encounter but leave everything else alone. We don't have Hazmat suits since that would slow us down. Whoever comes in behind us will have to clear the building of any contaminants, but that's a problem for another day. Our mission is to extricate Ava as quickly as possible."

"Understood," Sam said, the others murmuring in agreement.

"Jett will update the embassy only after we've gone wheel's up. We don't want any complications if they attempt to get involved in Ava's rescue. Aside from Ava and Badr's men, no one else should be in the warehouse."

Sam crossed his arms, looking down at the map. "If we're followed as we leave, we can detour through the city rather than jumping on the highway. It will be easier to lose them with all the turns and won't delay us too much in getting to the airport."

"Agreed," Nick said, glancing down at the map. "It won't be a problem. I've got all the possible routes marked. We'll get Ava and get the hell out of Egypt—assuming her health allows for her to travel."

"If she requires medical treatment, we'll have to bring her to the embassy," Luke admitted. "They're in the dark at the moment, however, and it will be tricky explaining why we're there. Jett can smooth things over, but heading there will be our last resort. Does anyone have any questions?"

"No." Sam's gaze landed on the body armor and weapons neatly arranged on the beds. Ava's belongings were off to the side, along with the men's rucksacks. It twisted Sam's gut to see her hot pink suitcase. She'd wheeled that into the lobby in Mexico only a couple of months ago. It had been in her hotel room in Paris. He couldn't imagine a world where Ava's things existed and she was simply gone. They'd save her. They had to, because the alternative was unthinkable.

"I'll load her belongings into one of the SUVs," Gray said, following Sam's gaze. "Now that we've got two vehicles, there's no sense in circling back here to retrieve anything."

"We aren't staying in Egypt any longer than we have to," Luke agreed. Sam clenched his fist. The only way they'd be staying longer was if Ava was hurt or their mission failed.

Gray crossed the room, grabbing the suitcase in one hand and hefting the box up with his other arm. They'd have to descend down the back stairwell so as not to arouse suspicion when the entire team departed. Their rucksacks and gear might be explained by their cover of traveling through Egypt, but the hot pink suitcase stood out. They'd checked over their weapons earlier in the hotel room, ensuring everything was in working order, but those would need to be concealed to exit the building.

"Grab your gear, boys," Luke said, and the men hustled over to strap on their body armor and comms units. "We roll out in five."

***

Sam signaled to his teammates as they jogged down the block in Cairo late that night. They were close. So fucking close. He could almost taste the sweet victory of getting Ava back. His gaze swept the quiet street, dark buildings looming over them, a few cars parked on the side of the road. The night was

SAM

silent. Still. Moving through the shadows, they were the only ones out in this part of the city.

His earpiece crackled, and then he heard Nick's voice. "I'm in position. I left one SUV around the corner. I've got eyes on both buildings but can remain concealed from this location. Over."

"Roger that," Sam said.

"I've got you in my sights," Gray said over the comms units. "The second SUV is a block east, and I'm moving toward you. If we need to split up, we'll rendezvous at the airport later. I'll wait near the loading dock until you're in position before moving in."

"Copy that. Sam and I are moving along the east side of the warehouse," Luke said. "The street is clear. We'll be at the back door in one minute. Over."

Sam jogged with his rifle at the ready. Although the city block was quiet, there was no telling what types of surveillance cameras Badr had on his buildings. Just because they hadn't spotted an obvious one didn't mean they weren't being watched. They'd scouted the area hours ago during the light of day but didn't want to draw attention to themselves by lingering.

"I'm in position," Gray said a moment later.

Sam clicked on his mic. "Luke and I are approaching the back of the warehouse. Looks like it's just an emergency exit since the loading dock is on the east side. Should be fairly easy to breach." They crouched behind some bushes, moving closer.

"I don't see any cameras back here," Sam said. "Seems odd."

"It works to our advantage. They don't need to know that we're coming."

Adrenaline coursed through Sam's veins as they moved within ten feet of the exit. The lock would be easy enough to shoot out, but then the entire building would know they were here. They'd have to hustle once they were inside. "It's quiet," Sam murmured. "Too quiet."

"Or maybe it's our lucky day." Luke shot him a look and then clicked on his mic. "Sam and I are in position. We'll move on my count. Three. Two. One." Sam and Luke ran to the back door. With one quick gunshot, the lock was broken. Sam yanked the heavy door open as the fire alarm sounded. Flashing strobe lights lit the inner hallway, causing him to wince in his night-vision goggles.

"They triggered the alarm," Gray told Nick over the headsets. "Be prepared for company."

"I'm ready for those mofos," Nick said. "Looks like a light just went on in the office building across the street. Somebody's up now."

"Fuck," Sam ground out. "Now they all know that we're here." He and Luke jogged down the hallway, their thumping footsteps concealed by the piercing alarm. A door opened to the right, a man stepping out, and Luke lifted his rifle, taking a single shot.

The man fell to the ground, and they jogged by the body, only briefly looking into the room the man had come from. It was empty.

"Turn left at the end of the hall," Luke said. "When West sent over the building schematics, the largest room was there. That's probably where they're building the sculptures."

"Ava could be anywhere," Sam said, his heart pounding.

"We'll start there and then search the entire

SAM

warehouse if necessary. We're not leaving without her."

***

Ava jolted awake, her heart racing as the fire alarm sounded in the building. She lifted a hand above her eyes, squinting at the bright light. She'd fallen asleep in the corner again, although this time she was all alone in the large workroom. Ava knew a man stood guard outside the locked door. She'd heard him talking earlier, but he'd eventually gone quiet. Badr had offered her nothing aside from bread and water, but at least she wasn't tied up or injured.

The only time they'd allowed her to leave the room was to use the bathroom down the hall. She hadn't been able to see much either—just a long corridor, with doors shut on either side. If she'd run, she'd have been quickly stopped. If she'd attempted to fight, Ava knew she'd have been harmed.

Rising to her feet, she blinked, looking at the table. The second sculpture she'd finished late this evening was gone. It wasn't very intricate but served Badr's purposes. She hated knowing something beautiful she'd created would be used to cause harm. He'd probably already had chemicals hidden inside her newest piece. Fear suddenly twisted inside her. What if there was a fire from whatever materials he'd been storing? There was still a chemical scent in the air, although she'd grown used to it, no longer sneezing all the time. She sniffed the air now, not smelling any smoke yet. Worry washed over her. No one had shut off the fire alarm yet, and the piercing sound and flashing strobe lights were making her head hurt. The doorknob rattled, and then the man who'd been guarding her burst into the room. He looked up at the fire alarm and then motioned for her to come with him. "Let's go! Hurry!" The man lifted his phone to his ear, yelling rapidly in Arabic as she quickly crossed the room.

Badr's men had left nothing but the sheets of metal in here, and her guard would see if she grabbed one in attempt to defend herself. Still, Ava's gaze swept the room anyway, desperate, but there was nothing else. Another man was yelling in the hallway as she moved through the doorway, and then Ava shrieked as she heard a gunshot. Jumping back, she tried to close the door behind her to take cover, but the guard pushed it open, forcing his way inside.

A second gunshot sounded, resounding through the halls of the warehouse, and Ava cowered on the ground. Her guard was fumbling with the doorknob but couldn't lock it from the inside. If the shooter came in here, they'd be killed.

For a split second, Ava wondered if she was being rescued, then quickly quashed that idea. It hadn't been long enough for anyone to fly over here and locate her. Maybe Sam was able to get in contact with someone in Egypt, but even if so, she'd been kidnapped from her apartment. She wasn't being held in one of Badr's office buildings downtown. Did anyone even know about this place? She wished she'd texted Sam or Wren some information about it when she'd first started on the sculptures. They'd have no way of knowing where specifically in Cairo she was. Tears smarted her eyes as her guard began yelling in Arabic, frantically pushing the door shut.

Ava would die here before she ever saw her family,

friends, or Sam again.

The fire alarm stopped as suddenly as it had started, the silence deafening. Ava covered her ears, still feeling them ring.

Another shot rang out, and then a muffled voice was yelling on the other side of the door. She instinctively moved back, trying to get away, and then two men came bursting inside, the guard falling to the floor from the momentum. Ava screamed as he was shot mere feet away from her, blood pooling on the ground beside him. She stumbled to her feet, and then one of the men was ripping off his helmet and night vision goggles, calling out her name. Ava's heart stopped as Sam's green eyes bore into hers. Time seemed to stand still, the chaos around them pausing, and then she was running to him, throwing herself into his arms. Sam hefted her up, holding her tightly as she wrapped her arms and legs around him, clinging to him desperately. She could hear Luke talking into his microphone and vaguely noticed him taking Sam's rifle.

"We've secured the package," Luke said in a clipped tone. "Repeat. We've secured the package. Prepare to move out."

"Are you hurt?" Sam asked, one big hand running over the back of her head, cupping it as she cried into his neck.

"No," she whimpered. "I'm fine. Get me out of here."

"You're safe," he murmured as Luke continued to update the rest of the team. "We've got a plane ready to go. We're going to exit the building, hustle down the block to the SUVs, and then head straight to the airport. Gray and Nick are here, too. We've got you."

"Okay. Okay," she said, lifting her head to look right at him. Their faces were inches apart, and Sam was the best thing she'd ever seen. His strength and scent surrounded her, his strong arms holding her tightly. Ava looked right into his concerned eyes, seeing the worry reflected in them. "You came for me," she said, her voice wobbly.

"Of course I did, princess," Sam replied, his voice thick with emotion. "You already knew I was coming to take you home. I'd have gone anywhere to get you back. You're it for me. We'll do things the right way this time around, but I already know that I'm not letting you go."

"I'm not letting you go either," she said fiercely, tears streaming down her cheeks.

He shifted one hand, thumbing them away. "Don't cry," he murmured, and his deep voice soothed something inside her, filled her with something she hadn't even realized she'd needed. Even in this damn warehouse she felt safe just being in his arms.

"I'm okay. I'm okay now," she said, wiping away her tears as Sam gently wrapped his own hand around hers. He was being so damn careful with her. It made Ava want to cry all over again from an emotion she couldn't even express.

"Then let's roll out of here and get you home," he said, gently setting her on her feet. "You can call Wren from the airplane and tell her the news yourself." She bit her lip and nodded tearfully, looking up at him, and then Sam was kissing her, somehow both sweet and fierce. Gray cleared his throat from the doorway. She didn't even know when he'd appeared, but the sound of gunshots had stopped. Luke was standing by as well, but she didn't

SAM

miss the tug of a smile on his lips.

Luke clicked his mic again. "Nick, we're ready to move out." He lifted his hand to his earpiece, and Ava assumed their teammate was replying.

"Let's go," Sam said, nodding toward the door. He took his rifle back then turned to her. "You okay to walk out of here, princess?"

"More than okay now that you're here." Their eyes locked for a beat longer, and then they were hustling down the hallway, Sam's arm wrapped around her. She squeezed her eyes shut as they passed several bodies on the floor, knowing Sam would get her around them. He shoved open the side door to a loading dock, Luke and Gray flanking them with their rifles raised. Then Sam was rushing her out into the dark night as the others provided cover, and as he pulled her close, Ava knew she was finally free.

Chapter 23

Ava sat snuggled against Sam on the flight back, her relief tangible. She'd slept for most of the trip, warm and content. The rest of the men had been talking quietly, but Sam had been happy to stay at her side. She'd put on one of his big sweatshirts over her camisole, breathing in his clean, musky scent. It almost felt like a dream of sorts—like she wasn't really here on an airplane, safe in his arms. Like the man who'd disappeared a year ago wasn't holding her carefully, acting as if Ava was the most important thing in the world to him.

"You doing okay, princess?" he asked, his lips brushing against her hair. It was comforting, and she relaxed further against him, enjoying the feel of Sam's muscular body. It wasn't sexual, just safe. For the first time in her life, she felt like she was exactly where she was supposed to be—with him, heading home.

"I'm okay. I still can't believe the past few days were even real. It feels like a dream—a nightmare. I

SAM

was supposed to be having the summer of my life, and I ended up getting kidnapped in a foreign country. I was so stupid going there without looking into my employer."

"No," he soothed. "You're not stupid. You took what sounded like an amazing opportunity. No one would have expected something like this. No one," he stressed. "You're a talented artist and will have so many more amazing chances to prove exactly that. Just promise me next time you jet off somewhere you'll at least give me the names of some people or tell me where you're staying."

Ava squeezed him tightly. "Promise. I don't think I'll be doing much traveling in the near future. I need some downtime to figure out what I want to do next. Wren was crying so much when I called her," she added. "I feel bad she had to worry about me like that not long after dealing with her sister."

"The world can be a crazy, dangerous place," Sam replied in a low voice.

She looked up at him, shocked by the intensity of his green gaze. "I still can't believe you found me," she said softly.

"You're not getting rid of me that easily," he joked before brushing back a strand of her hair. They'd kissed briefly in the warehouse, but this felt different. He ducked down and kissed her gently, reverently, holding her close in his strong arms. Ava felt a blush spreading across her cheeks, and he smiled. "I know you're not shy, princess. Is this just because the guys are around?"

"Sort of. I'm mostly embarrassed your team had to come rescue me."

"I'd do it again if it meant keeping you safe," Sam

said, a catch in his voice. "Besides, this is what we do. Evil is lurking everywhere. You do what you can to avoid it, but sometimes people are caught in situations they never expected to be."

"What's going to happen when we get home?" Ava asked. "Are we landing upstate near Shadow Security's headquarters?"

"We are. I'll drive you back to your place in the city if you like, or you're welcome to stay with me for a while to decompress. It's safe there, and I'll get some time off, so you won't be alone. We never actually had any down time after our last op," he admitted.

"Geez, that's right. I've sort of lost track of time what with everything that happened," she said. "You called me as soon as you were back in the States." Ava's fingers trailed down his forearm. His flesh was warm, but Sam was solid muscle beneath. She wanted to soothe him, too. He'd dealt with one stressful situation after another, putting his life on the line to save her. "I'm sure you're exhausted. I don't even know how to thank you for risking everything to come save me."

"You don't need to thank me," Sam assured her, putting one big hand over her own. He squeezed it gently, his thumb caressing her skin, and the touch sent shivers racing down her spine. Sam might be big and strong, but he was always so careful with her. "I'll crash after I make sure you're settled in," he said, "wherever you decide to stay. The rest of the guys will meet with Jett after we land. I'll debrief with him in a day or so. You're my priority right now."

Tears smarted her eyes as she looked up at him again. "Hey," he said huskily, gently wiping away a

SAM

stray teardrop. "Please don't cry."

"I was afraid I'd never get out of there," she admitted. "Mohammad said I needed to create the sculptures for him or he'd pass me around to his men."

Sam stiffened, his muscles going tense around her. "I want to kill that bastard."

"I guess he wasn't one of the men you guys hurt," Ava replied. Maybe she should be frightened that Sam and his teammates had easily taken the lives of the people who'd kidnapped her, but those men were pure evil. Aside from threatening her, they planned to harm hundreds of other people. Maybe thousands. She couldn't be scared of Sam or his teammates. They were all alpha males, protectors, who'd saved her and helped to rid the world of evil men.

"No, he wasn't there. I would've loved to take that fucker out for putting you in that situation. He won't be a free man for long. We'll be giving a full report to the Feds about the terror plot. I can't usually discuss classified information with you, but you unfortunately know a significant amount about this one. If and when you're feeling up for it, it'd be helpful to give the government a sketch of the sculptures you made so they know what to be looking for. As of right now, Badr still has plans to move them into the States."

"Of course. I can draw some sketches of them. I feel terrible that I was even involved in it."

"Not your fault," Sam assured her. "You had no choice in the matter, and you did what you could to survive and stay safe until I could get to you." He glanced up as one of his teammates came down the aisle of the plane, and then Luke was standing before them.

"ETA is two hours. We'll touch down in New York and get you on your way. I understand you don't need immediate medical attention, Ava, but we can arrange for you to meet with someone, if you'd like to talk about what you went through."

"I'll be okay for now," Ava assured him. "I just want to sleep for a day or two."

"We'll get some names to you just in case. I'm sure Sam told you he'll get you home. Wren wanted me to make sure to let you know you'd be welcome to stay with us if you like. Wherever you prefer."

Ava glanced at Sam, hesitant. "I might stay at Sam's place a few days, then head back into the city. I'm not sure I want to be alone just yet."

Sam leaned down and kissed the top of her head. "You're safe with me," he murmured, his thumb gently rubbing the nape of her neck. She relaxed into him again, content. It shouldn't feel so good to be in his arms, but she couldn't deny that it just seemed right.

"Good choice," Luke said, his lips quirking. "And if I didn't say it before, Ava, we're all relieved as hell that you're okay."

Nick hustled down the aisle of the plane just then, talking quietly on his cell phone as he moved away from the others for privacy.

"What's that about?" Luke asked, his gaze tracking after him.

Sam lifted a shoulder. "It's about that old girlfriend of his. He didn't say what's going on but seems worked up about it." Ava watched as Nick sat down in a seat away from everyone else.

"Well, I just wanted to check in," Luke said. "I'll let you relax. Let me know if you need anything.

SAM

We're glad to have you back." He turned and walked away, leaving the two of them alone once more.

"You should rest," Sam said gently. "I know you're exhausted."

"Maybe I just like talking with you," she said sleepily, but Ava couldn't stop the yawn that came anyway.

"We'll have plenty of time to talk, princess. I already told you I'm going to do things the right way this time around. I'll probably be watching you so carefully from now on, you'll be the one ghosting me," he said with a wink.

"Never," she said, hugging him again as she relaxed into his big body.

"Thank God. I'd respect your wishes if you didn't want to give this a chance, but I can't imagine my life without you in it." His lips brushed against the top of her head again, and she snuggled into him, content to be safe in his arms.

Epilogue

One month later

Ava smiled as they finished dinner at Jett and Anna's house, Sam's chair close to hers, his arm draped protectively around her shoulders. There was laughter and conversation floating throughout the large home, and it felt good to be surrounded by people who had become family. Jett's assistant Lena had cooked a delicious multi-course meal, and the entire team had come for dinner to celebrate Ava's rescue and the thwarting of Badr's terror plot. The FBI had intercepted the sculptures when they arrived on a plane at JFK last week, and the entire situation was now behind them.

The group rose and moved to the kitchen, helping to clear the table before dessert. Ford was beside Clara, Luke with Wren, and Gray stood alone, taking a pull of his beer. Only Nick looked slightly stressed out, and Ava wondered what was going on. He'd been texting someone on his phone earlier but hadn't

SAM

shared any details.

Jett strode in carrying his and Anna's plates, and Ava watched as he ducked and pressed a kiss to Anna's temple. It was sweet and chaste but made Ava long for exactly that—a gruff, alpha male who doted on his other half, happy in their home together, and surrounded by friends. Sam had more than proven himself to be an excellent boyfriend over the past month, and although she hadn't officially moved into his house, she spent most nights there. Her days were filled with painting, lost in her art, while he took new missions with the Shadow Ops Team.

Sam took the plates from Jett, stacking them in the sink as Lena pulled a cake from the oven. She set it on the counter to cool, turning to stir melted chocolate in a saucepan.

"Oh my gosh, the cake and chocolate sauce smell incredible," Anna said. "You always outdo yourself, Lena!"

"I'm quite certain we'd be lost without her," Jett agreed.

Gray was watching Lena closely and moved to help get dessert plates from the cupboard. Ava always considered him to be the strong, silent type, but it was interesting to see the way he kept his eyes on Jett's personal assistant.

"Who doesn't love chocolate sauce?" Lena asked, moving efficiently around the kitchen.

Ava looked across the room at Sam and winked. She'd turned him into her own decadent dessert last night, painting a chocolate heart with an arrow through it on his abdomen. The heart had been askew, the arrow pointing down his happy trail, leading straight to the erection that had been standing loud and proud.

After Ava had licked off every last drop, he'd flipped her over, taking her from behind as he'd wrapped one hand in her strawberry-blonde hair and sunk deep inside her body, his lips at her neck, his cock thrusting in and out. Her mewls of pleasure had gotten louder and louder until she'd been crying out his name, unable to stop the waves of ecstasy washing over her.

Sam had kissed his way down her back afterwards, gentle and sweet, then held her in place as he licked and laved at her pussy from behind, making her orgasm yet again. She shivered at the memory, and Sam prowled across the room toward her, taking her hand in his and lowering his mouth to her ear. "Tonight, I'm painting you, my little vixen," he said huskily. "I'm going to taste every inch of you."

"Promise?" she teased, turning her head to meet his heated gaze.

"Guaranteed."

She smiled as he ducked for a kiss, warmth and arousal flooding through her. Ava's satisfaction was always guaranteed when she was with Sam, and she loved all the different ways that he could make her come apart in his arms. "Do you two need a room?" Anna joked as she moved past them. "We could probably use some more Shadow Ops babies around here."

"Anna," Jett muttered, but his eyes shone with amusement as they followed his fiancée's movements around the kitchen.

"What?" Ava joked. "Your two won't be enough, Anna?"

Anna looked pointedly at Ford and Clara, her eyes

SAM

twinkling in amusement. "I don't know. There might be more on the way."

"Guess the cat's out of the bag," Clara said as she flushed. "I told Anna the other day that I'm pregnant but didn't know how or when to make an announcement. She promised to do the honors when the time was right."

"You're welcome," Anna teased.

Ford ducked down and kissed his wife, beaming, as the rest of the room erupted in surprise.

"Wait, you two?" Gray asked. "Damn. I don't even have a woman, and everyone here is getting hitched and having kids."

"Not everyone," Ava said with a laugh. "Even I don't rush into things that quickly."

"Maybe someday," Sam offered, winking at her.

After everyone congratulated Ford and Clara, they had dessert and laughed more over the next hour. Ava glanced out the back doors when they were done eating, noticing the full moon. She slipped outside as Sam was helping to clean up, enjoying the peacefulness of the night.

"What are you staring so hard at?" Sam asked softly as he joined her on the back deck of Jett's house a few minutes later.

"This place has great lines. Look at the slope of the rooftop. It's strong but a nice contrast to the forest and trees. And silhouetted by the full moon like that? It's hauntingly beautiful."

"I'm sure Jett would let you set up an easel out here sometime and paint. Just don't let them rope you into diaper duty," Sam joked.

Ava shuddered. "Goodness, no. I'll watch my own babies someday, but other people's children? No thanks."

Sam's husky laughter filled the air. It felt intimate to be out here alone in the quiet night. They'd made love almost every night since they'd gotten back together, but tonight felt different, like the start of something serious. Something more. "So you want kids." It wasn't a question.

She shot him a look. "Of course. Two point five, plus a dog or something. A husband."

"Any idea who the lucky guy might be?" he teased.

Ava winked. "I don't know. You gotta play your cards right, soldier."

"Tough crowd," he chuckled. "Hopefully you're not still after some Frenchman," he growled, moving closer and stealing a kiss. He kept her in his arms, and she snuggled closer to him.

"Nope. I gave up on that dream long ago. I could paint this someday," she said, bringing the conversation back around full circle.

"You could. Your paintings are amazing, princess. Like I told the guys, I can paint a wall a solid color, but that's about it." His lips quirked.

"I don't know," she teased. "You wielded a paintbrush in Paris."

Sam's eyes lit up. "I meant what I said earlier. Tonight, I'm painting all over your gorgeous curves and then tasting every part of you," he said, pulling her in for another slow, heated kiss. His fingers tangled in her hair, and one hand slid down to her ass, squeezing possessively. Ava pressed closer, feeling his erection against her stomach. She shamelessly rubbed herself against him, teasing. Sam growled and then lifted her into his arms as she squealed in surprise. "You're trouble, princess," he said, his voice thick

SAM

with desire.

"You must bring it out in me," she said innocently.

He chuckled, but then his eyes grew serious. "Maybe so, but you're it for me. Someday I want all of this with you—the house, the kids, the wedding."

"Are you asking me to marry you?" she said, trying to hide her smile.

"Well, I planned to get you a ring first," he admitted.

"Yes. I'll marry you," she declared, and Sam laughed again as he nuzzled his face against hers, sending warmth coursing through her entire body. His lips pressed against her cheek.

"Always the impulsive one," he said, but she could feel him smiling.

"You love that about me."

His eyes met hers again. "I love everything about you. Your smile, your sense of humor, the way you feel in my arms. The way you look in my bed. I love you, Ava Kincaid. I want to spend forever with you."

Tears shone in her eyes as she tried to contain all the emotions welling up within her. "I love you, too, Sam. So much. I never thought the guy I met in Paris would be the man I spend the rest of my life with, but I want that, too. Us. Forever. I'm not letting you get away from me again."

"Then marry me," he said huskily. "We'll go pick out a ring together this weekend."

"Yes," she whispered. "Of course, I'll marry you."

He kissed her again, deeply, under the full moon, their friends inside of the laughter-filled home. It was the start of something amazing, a life spent together, and a future brighter than either of them could have dreamed.

About the Author

USA Today Bestselling Author Makenna Jameison writes sizzling romantic suspense, including the addictive Alpha SEALs series.

Makenna loves the beach, strong coffee, red wine, and traveling. She lives in Washington DC with her husband and two daughters.

Visit www.makennajameison.com to discover your next great read.

Manufactured by Amazon.ca
Acheson, AB